I0538773

Glass Eater

a novel by

Dan Coffey

Rocket Science Press
SHIPWRECKT BOOKS PUBLISHING COMPANY

IN®
DIE

Minnesota

Cover art: *Tower of Babel* by Pieter Bruegel the Elder (1563).
Cover and interior design by Shipwreckt Books.

Contents

Introduction by Richard Nixon

You know me, probably too well; nevertheless, let me introduce myself again. I am Richard Milhous Nixon. Although most people assume I died long ago, the fact is that I continue to live, in a manner both grotesque and difficult to fathom. True, I am but a misshapen blob in a laboratory setting, but I can still be counted among the living.

This life of ours is not a popularity contest. We are here for a reason. Each of us has a destiny, and some of us share the same one, though we may be the last to realize it.

At the risk of alienating my few fans, I want to remind you that no one of us is really in charge of much. We are all subjects of a Higher Power; the one I choose to call *Jesus*. Yes, we Quakers believe in Jesus, at least those of us who have not blended in with the Unitarian Universalists and other Ban the Bomb types who have eschewed a theology of any kind and now only want to protest Monsanto products.

This war we are engaged in, and yes, it is a real war, with heavy casualties on all sides, is not going to go away merely because some find it inconvenient or an assault on their sensibilities. This fight predated my entry into politics and it will continue after I finally melt and drip off the laboratory shelf. It may even be an extension of that heavenly battle, which Milton described in his twin volumes, one of which he wrote when he was already totally blind, and had to memorize the day's writing in

1

order to dictate it to his daughter when she came to feed him his dinner at night.

You are surprised that I am an educated man. I am nothing if not clever, and sensitive to a fault. That sensitivity made me want to be liked, to be a chum among chums, a fellow well-met, and when that didn't happen I became bitter and vengeful. End of story.

But I am not an especially bad man. Nor are the men I surrounded myself with in the past. Nor are my current companions, Kissinger and Hoover. Together we enjoy an extended twilight brought about by modern science. We want you to think of us as your elder brothers who have gone ahead to make smooth the path for the rest of you.

Yes, I sabotaged the peace talks with North Viet Nam because I didn't want Johnson getting credit for ending Kennedy's war, and I didn't want that blithering idiot Humphrey to stand a chance of beating me to the Presidency. Yes, I was petty and venal, dishonest and manipulative. What politician isn't?

You know who was an even bigger asshole than me? Reagan. He was as bad as they get, and such a smooth-talking blowhard that he spent his second term with full-blown Alzheimer's, though nobody dared say so. If my sin involved being too clever, then Reagan's sin can be ascribed to his massive stupidity. The man was actually borderline retarded. His first wife Jane Wyman divorced him after she discovered the depths of his dullness, and his second wife Nancy didn't care, because she enjoyed being the brains of the outfit.

This story you're about to read involves a man you've never heard of, the Glass Eater. I only just learned of his existence, and not because he represents anything extraordinary in these times. He is a man of dubious character who has bumbled through his life like millions of others, seeking to avoid real work and to slide by whenever possible.

Men whose opinion I trust have counseled me that we should appreciate and encourage men like him, just

2

because they are so unexceptional. If we had more garden-variety men in government, we might actually keep this thing afloat a while longer. Maybe that's the real advantage of Democracy. It's like the police exam. They reject you if your IQ is too high. Men who are too smart are always questioning the rules instead of following them. We don't want creative police. We want police who respect the law. The writing of laws is left to a different kind of person altogether.

The reason that the Negros don't follow the rules is because they don't feel they had any hand in writing them, and they're right. So, you end up with these do-gooder liberals like Kennedy and Humphrey, who take it upon themselves to make it all better, but they can't. Our leaders are forced to take charge of a divided society, one that's not going to get better before it gets worse.

Our prisons are full of Negroes, not because our justice system is flawed, but because it is the Negroes who commit most of the crimes. Nobody wants to say it, but those in our judicial system know this to be the case. We've inherited an untenable society, a government that can't be honest because nobody wants to deal with the truth. Yes, I was a liar. So was every President we've ever had.

The Glass Eater is a white man. He is therefore predisposed to feeling like a participant in the social contract. His people are in charge, and as long as he doesn't openly defy authority, he has a good chance of getting away with whatever he wants to get away with. Sure, he can mess up, but from what I've heard, he's too slick an operator to want to risk being imprisoned with a bunch of angry Niggers.

For the Negros, as well as for most of the rest of us, the fact is, it's the Jews who have us marching to the beat of *their* drum. Who do you think caused 9/11? Why did we invade Iraq? Why are we going to invade Syria and eventually Iran? Because the Jews want us to, that's why. But you probably already knew that. You just don't

3

want to admit it because then you'd have to do something about it, and you don't want to be bothered right now. You're kind of busy.

Maybe it's time to ask Jesus to step in and make things right before they get much worse. All the best people are coming to that conclusion. Even Henry, Dick and Don sometimes make rumblings in that direction. They're getting old and scared, too.

Me, I'm not afraid of anything or anybody.

Like John of Patmos said: "Come, Lord Jesus."

Like W said to Saddam, "Bring it on."

—Richard M. Nixon
Scripps Laboratory, Building B-2, La Jolla, California.

A Doctor's Opinion

I am personal physician to both Richard Nixon and Henry Kissinger. In that capacity, I've learned a great deal about the workings of these men's minds. I've also witnessed the inner workings of our government, especially the hidden decision-making that defies both the checks and the balances of our democratic system, as well as any common sense understanding of human behavior. These men are insane. Dangerously so. They should have been stopped long ago, but instead we use all the tools of modern medical science to keep them alive. I have been complicit in this and for that I am deeply ashamed.

My colleagues, other physicians of note who have also sold their souls and whatever integrity they may have held onto after a career ministering to heads of state, often tease me about my charges.

"Does Tricky Dick continue in his sly ways?" asks a distinguished Austrian doctor with a fragile command of our language. "Has Henry managed to broker any more fatuous peace accords?" he continues, smirking in that way only Europeans can.

We laugh, sip cognac, and fight down that rising tide of self-revulsion only true cowards know. Yes, we work for hypocrites and madmen. But let me tell you who the real master of that bunch is.

"Cheney," you proffer. "Wolfowitz," you volunteer. No, I'm here to tell you these were only the minions of the man whose grasp of the demonic is such that the scent of brimstone follows wherever he goes. It is

Rumsfeld who challenges Lucifer himself for the Keys to the Dark Kingdom.

Don the demon. Likeable, even believable. When Colin Powell lied about the weapons of mass destruction, Don was nearby him, relaxed and grinning. Whoever stepped up to the plate to trade his integrity for profit was handsomely rewarded. None of those guys need ever worry about money again.

Some of them probably don't sleep well. In their tortured dreams a million Iraqis howl for a vengeance that even a double dose of Ambien can't squelch.

But we healers can only heal so much, and even then, our cures are often as partial as they are temporary. We might do well to ask ourselves, are we in the presence of some supernatural force? Rather than personality quirks or insanity, are we instead dealing with evil?

It would seem in the case of Nixon *et al*, that we are dealing with Pure Evil, and upon closer analysis this is indeed the case. These men are each playing a role without being aware they could, if they wanted, stop acting at any time. They are like a pack of dogs who howl at sunset. If you could isolate each dog and ask him why he howls, he would be unable to answer the question. The wolf would not be aware that he was actually howling. He would admit to being aware of howling, but could not attest to his participation in the event. And as to why they were howling at all, well, that lay beyond his ken.

When Lieutenant William Calley and his men massacred an entire Vietnamese village of old people and children, how did the soldiers overcome their initial resistance to killing fellow humans? They simply made a mental decision to deny them their humanity. Sure, they resembled humans, and in fact southeast Asian babies looked a lot like the American soldiers' babies back home, but they were Viet Cong, and the threat of evil lay in the very fact that they so closely resembled humans. If they weren't Viet Cong, why would they be wearing black pajamas and cone-shaped straw hats?

6

Why were they here at all, instead of back home, where real humans lived, where the soldiers' own families lived, sitting in air-conditioned rooms watching television?

The path to evil is a short one, and can be traveled in a heartbeat, especially if one is not acting alone. Even that perpetual loner Nixon was not a lone instigator. He was part of a team. He probably even thought of himself as a good man, as God's servant, a Quaker trying his best to bring light into a dark world.

Groups often bring out the worst in us. A group of fifteen-year-old boys will have the emotional age of three-year-olds. They will engage in actions that are dangerous or cruel without a moment's forethought. Girls can be just as cruel, ganging up to pick on the weak and defenseless in their midst. Like chickens crammed in a small space, girls will gladly peck to death the weakest in their bunch.

In my opinion, Nixon and his cruel, seemingly evil friends do not think of themselves as bad men. They did not aspire to evil; but achieved evil through exceptional lack of vigilance mixed with common arrogance. Insane? Always. Evil? Sometimes.

The subject of this book, the persona who shares his story with us, this Glass Eater, is no better or worse than his tormenters. The world is now full of men like him who have moved abroad for economic reasons and find becoming slowly unglued not an unpleasant outcome. They are like college boys who began to cut their classes and found no real consequence to doing so. As lazy as they are naughty, they learn that boredom finds a cure in simple movement. Drifting from one impoverished corner of the globe to another, they leave no wake behind because they matter to no one. As clients of hotels, restaurants, bars and massage parlors, they will scarcely be noticed, much less missed, when they move on. When they die, their embassy will attempt to contact relatives, and finding none, consign them to a pauper's grave.

7

M E M O
Our kind of people?

From: Henry Kissinger
To: Richard M. Nixon

I have been made aware of an American citizen who is our kind of guy, a man who is not afraid to stretch the truth if it fits his plans for a better world. We should find a way to get him on our side. He makes his living eating ashtrays, but has been employed in the past as a multi-faceted con-man, swindling old ladies and the like. The perfect diplomat!

His powers of persuasion are considerable, and he quickly develops an emotional bond with his victims. The depth of that bond does not depend on the amount of money involved in the scam, but rather is a means in itself. He manipulates others out of loneliness. He is a vampire who feeds on trust instead of blood.

Again, he is surprisingly good at what he does, and with the right training and incentives, could join our side. What we have accomplished in Viet Nam, in Chile, and in Pakistan, he could emulate in our future endeavors, even though most of us old-timers are retired from public service.

We know otherwise, eh Richard? The good fight never ends, and this man could be a warrior. Like Oswald, he was married to a Russian!

It's hard to find a man who will willingly do the wrong thing for the right reasons. Most of us are weak and selfish. But here is such a man, and if he could be inspired to join a team effort and brave the ethical crowd, the namby-pamby do-gooders, we could be much more effective. We could change the world for the better, for good.

9

No more slip sliding. No more two steps forward and three back.

Now that you and I are well past our prime, we should be developing a protégé, someone we can count on to pull hard for the long haul. I remember myself as a young man, full of a desperate need to be recognized, and constantly searching for a situation in which I could prove my abilities. Surely these young men exist today. Perhaps our friend is one of them.

We who have been unafraid to risk the disapproval and even contempt of our constituency have had to develop thick skins when dealing with the press. Public opinion cannot be counted on. The approval of others is too fickle a base on which to build the city on a hill which will shine its light to inspire and comfort the lumpen proletariat below.

Most Americans are content to live in trailer parks and public housing. They will not grumble too loudly if given their daily dose of television and junk food. This man is one of us. He will not rest until his home is perched on the highest crag, until he is gnawing contentedly on freshly killed meat.

A true man develops his character by overcoming difficulty. A wimp finds temporary refuge in a philosophy that confuses its romantic goals and foolish assumptions with reality. Allende was such a wimp. We were proud to point this out, even though we could not openly be seen to oppose him. Pinochet took care of business for us because he was a real man, not afraid to be despised by wimps.

History may or may not remember us fondly. We don't give a shit.

1. Chowing Down on Broken Glass

I eat glass for a living. For the last couple of years, this has involved eating a glass ashtray each evening. I get the other men along the bar to wager that I can't eat an entire ashtray in one sitting. It takes me a couple of hours to do so, but I smash that ashtray into small shards and then slowly swallow them all. For this, I make anywhere from sixty to one hundred fifty dollars a night, tax free. It's a tough job, but somebody's got to do it. At least I've got to do something, and this is the best way to make money I've found recently.

I once met a man who ate an entire automobile. It took him almost two years to do so. He died shortly after swallowing the last bolt, but the autopsy revealed eating the car was not his undoing. It was liver cancer, an infirmity that had been progressing for some time.

My line of work proves one thing: that you can accomplish any seemingly impossible task if you first break it into small enough pieces and refuse to give up no matter how long it takes.

My wife is the unusual one in our family. She has a tattoo that stretches from her left shoulder to her right calf. I don't care much for tattoos, but I have to admit this one is well done, with all the colors and lines clear and defined. There is, however, the troubling issue of the name of her beloved at the time of the procedure. The first man was named Hugh, which was skillfully redrawn to read Bart, then Burt, then Bert. For a while she had a thing for men whose first names began with the letter "B." The moniker remains Bert to this day, as

11

the skin in that area was beginning to thin which permitted no more adjustment. Now, just above her buttocks surrounded by palm leaves, it reads "Bert," though she is now my wife and my name is Donald.

We have learned to accept each other with all our foibles. She is married to a man who eats ground glass for a living. I admit to myself that in her massage practice she sometimes strays over the line of what might be thought of as common decency. We each mind our own business.

The State of Emergency has been renewed again. I can't remember how many times they've said they're about to take away the curfew and stop interning the undesirables, but then they go and renew it for another ninety days and the undesirables stay where they are in those FEMA camps. The Swat Teams are still coming and going, especially downtown, running in and out of local businesses and dragging more undesirables away to the huge, black trucks, the ones they park out back with the engines running.

Things could be worse. They say that almost everyone in Western Africa has already died of Ebola. The government channel keeps repeating that only because of rapid action by our peacekeeping forces, we're spared the ionizing radiation that took out so much of Korea and Pakistan. So, we're luckier than some, I guess. I've heard the Zika problem in Brazil has peaked in intensity, and that the survivors all enjoy natural immunity. The population will recover within a century or two.

I'd like to think that my line of work has protected me from disease. Quite a few of my friends have died in the past few years, but I seem to enjoy better health as time passes. Maybe there's something in the glass they use to make ashtrays that is beneficial, some sort of micro-nutrient. The guy who ate the car didn't get cured of his cancer, but maybe if he'd have stuck with ashtrays he would have been. Just a thought. Sometimes it pays to stick with something, so matter how sick of it you've become.

A few years ago, I went to the emergency room because I had a terrific headache. They ran about fifteen thousand dollars' worth of tests and finally told me I had a brain tumor. I laughed and walked out the door. Good luck getting me to pay. If they're right, I'd be insane to give them my money now when the debt will dissolve the moment I die. If they're wrong, then why should I pay them for a faulty diagnosis? The headache went away as soon as I had a couple of cups of coffee. Quitting caffeine is really difficult. That's why I have no intention of trying it again.

The more coffee I drink, the more quick-witted and talkative I become. There's a point where I can't think or talk any faster, and then I nosedive into agonizing anxiety. You'd think I'd quit, or at least moderate, but such notions are foreign to my very nature. If it's worth doing, it's worth doing all the way, until I just can't do it anymore.

My wife and I only have sex once a year, on her birthday. To get herself in the mood she starts drinking at breakfast. By noon, she is no longer herself, adopting the character of Bette Davis, the thirties/forties film star. Even though English is not her first language, she does a very convincing impersonation, excelling especially in surveying the room and then proclaiming, "what a dump!" Unfortunately, by evening she has taken the role too far, and all the fun is gone. Unfortunately, that is when she decides to get physical. Our little game evolved from repeated viewings of our favorite Davis film, The Bride Came C.O.D.

In one scene, Jimmy Cagney, an aviator who has discovered that Davis is a rich heiress, conspires to trap her in a cave until he can claim the ransom from her rich father. By kissing him, she tastes that he has been out of the cave and eaten something, so she realizes she has been deceived, and begins hitting him furiously. That's my wife's favorite part of the movie. It was once ours, until she took it as license and inspiration to attack me like a polecat, all in the name of fun.

13

We have repeated this scenario *ad nauseam*. At this point in the birthday revelry, she has dropped the Bette Davis accent and is simply grunting and howling in her native Russian. It was fun the first year. By now, like those Twilight vampire films, this drama has grown tired through repeated sequels. This last time, she stayed drunk for three days, coming to when she stopped mid-sentence while telling a story at a dinner we were having with friends. She had been talking in a pirate voice, a cartoonish characterization full of swearing and fake Cockney nautical phrases, when all of a sudden she asked in all seriousness, "Where are we? What time is it? What are you doing here?" Needless to say, this Oscar-winning performance put a damper on the evening and our guests soon found an excuse to check on the baby sitter.

But we're happy most of the time. I never told her about my diagnosis of a brain tumor, but I'm saving that in case I need a "get out of jail" card to get her to cut me some slack. Not all my behavior is blameless, and every once in a while, I might need to get out of a jam by pointing out that although I am a flawed human being, I'm no sociopath either.

For most of my work life I worked in the furnace repair business. During that time, I never repaired a furnace, but rather gave the illusion of having done so, taking advantage of the fact that the obituary columns of local newspapers gave me plenty of leads to visit recent widows about to endure their first winter alone. I would arrive at the house announcing that I was the man who had installed this furnace and was here to check the inverter-combobulator before winter set in. Usually I would bring along a good-looking young man as my assistant. He would ask the widow about her late husband, their children, and generally charm her and soothe her fears. She would always confide that she knew nothing about the furnace for that had been part of her late husband's domain.

14

I would bang around on the pipes in the basement for a few minutes, then come upstairs holding a filthy piece of equipment that I had surreptitiously brought with me in the first place, and proclaim that this was her lucky day because if she had fired that baby up it would have been sure to blow the house sky-high. These invertor-combobulators usually run 700-800 bucks, but I had one in the truck that I would let her have for 350 cash, installation at no charge.

Nine out of ten times it worked and in the spring I could reprise the act again only with a roof repair version. Again, my assistant would praise the beauty of her grandchildren while I stomped around on the roof. This time I replaced the gutter diverticulator, which had rotted clear through. Usually I could only get two hundred for one of those imaginary babies, because the onset of winter is a lot scarier for most widows than is the beginning of summer.

When I tired of this, and when the complaints reached the local police, I would move to another community with a large percentage of recent widows in their own homes, and harsh winters. The lower the average temperature, the higher my profits. The northern Midwest was truly my field of dreams.

But then I heard of a friend who was making great bucks running a modeling agency for teen-age girls in the Southwest. In this case, of course, their mothers were the marks, and all I had to do was supervise a pretty college-aged girl to work with the potential models. I dropped a lot of names and made many a vague allusion to showcases in Rio and Paris, but was careful to never make promises I could be held to. One of my greatest breakthroughs was a series of affirmations sent to the fifteen-year old girls on their cell phones. "If he thinks I'm pretty, then I am," was one of them. "My hairs smells terrific and I feel just as good," was another. We had a good time making those up over shots and chasers in the motel room one night. Every teenage girl's life centers around her cell phone, so when it talks to her, she listens.

The mothers paid one monthly fee for the instruction, another for photographs and video demos, and we were able to get a dollar a day per client for the affirmations. It sure beat banging furnace pipes in the basement.

Eventually I know that I'll have to settle on a line of work that pays into social security. Once, when I was in my twenties, I was traveling in Mexico and I came upon an old American man who was staying in the same cheap hotel as I. He had been running a fever for days and was trapped in his room, covered in blankets. I asked him if he'd seen a doctor. No, he had no money for that. Didn't he have social security? No, he'd been self-employed all his life. No family, no girlfriend. At the time, I remember thinking, "Note to future self: don't end up like him."

Now that the Department of Homeland Security has taken over all the local police departments, the War on the Homeless has taken on new vigor. I have no desire to spend my golden years interned in a camp in Utah or Nevada. I've heard rumors that there is a plan to send the Homeless and Undesirables to Paraguay, a country that has agreed to accept them for a fee, and them allow them to live in the Chaco, a region as difficult as any on the planet. Coincidentally, it's also where George W. Bush bought a hundred thousand acres of land just before he left office, in case he had to flee to a place with no extradition policy. Paraguay also welcomed many an ex-Nazi after World War II ended. The land-locked nation served as a sort of a second-tier Argentina.

Well, I always wanted an excuse to work on my Spanish. Maybe there would be an upside to being shipped off to *Nowhere Latin America*. Room and board would be paid for by FEMA or some other Federal Agency.

There's already a stretch of Federal land in the Colorado Desert, east of the Salton Sea, where a decommissioned army base, Slab City, is home to a great number of nearly homeless year-around, though the population swells during the winter and gets very small

16

during the summer, when the average temperature is 110 degrees. These people live in their vehicles and in tents. There is no water, electricity or sewer service, but the residents of Slab City make do.

There is another settlement nearby called East Jesus. People who live there are well aware of their predicament, and would rather choose freedom over the dubious comfort of charity.

Most migration is caused by economic incentives. Many of us are economic refugees, though we're often reluctant to admit it. The reason I don't live in downtown Manhattan isn't because I don't enjoy museums and restaurants, it's because I can't afford the rents. The reason I no longer live in the States is because it's too damn expensive for what you get.

After some Internet research, I found several affordable and interesting places I could live in South America and Southeast Asia. Looking at making a major move in order to free myself from the grind of trying to make ends meet gave me a sudden rush of hope. Unfortunately, my wife wasn't as hopeful. "What a dump!" she intoned, wearily, as she wandered around the kitchen, looking for something to eat. I knew she would probably find a foreign dump excessively dumpy.

We decided to try Nicaragua first, and then if that didn't seem like a practical home, we'd try Thailand. We bought tickets that very evening, but our mood as we did so was less than celebratory. I wasn't sure about Natasha's desire or motivation in this quest for change. In fact, wasn't sure she even wanted to be with me anymore, much less retire to a Banana Republic.

The morning we left, Natasha and I were hopeful for a few hours, until we were stopped at the airport. As we went through immigration, we were forcibly separated. They took each of us to small offices on either side of a hallway. I was detained only briefly, but she was in there for almost half an hour. When she emerged, she wouldn't look at me, but she did manage to say, "I'm not going," as she headed back to baggage claim. I chased her for a while, asking what happened and why had she changed her mind, but she was in no mood to respond. The last thing she said to me was, "Have a nice life."

It turns out I never made it to Nicaragua, or Thailand for that matter. They took me off the plane in Miami and gave me two men as escorts who sat with me in some sort of lounge that felt a lot like a jail. We watched TV together, *Fox and Friends*, as I recall. Then I saw my picture fill the screen with the caption, "ISIS terrorist captured at Miami airport." And then a segment where my wife was being interviewed by Sean Hannity and a blonde bimbo who pretended to be a tough-talking journalist unafraid to ask the important questions like, "What were my favorite TV shows and did I ever play video games and if so which ones?"

Hard-hitting journalism it wasn't, but my wife looked great under the TV lights. Then it occurred to me that this segment must have been recorded earlier, because she had had her hair styled in that way a couple of days ago. I asked my companion to the right if what we were watching was live TV, but he simply stared straight ahead, the only visible sign of life being the muscles in his jaw flexing as he slowly chewed gum. I suppose he had been instructed not to talk to me.

His companion also stared straight ahead, but at least he was watching TV, witnessing my wife telling the world that I was a high-ranking officer in ISIS, the spin-off terrorist group that split from Al-Qaida. He seemed interested in her tale of woe, and impressed by the variety of realistic details with which she embellished her story. At one point, she began to weep, then looked into the camera and sobbed, "He told me he was a chiro-practor. And I believed him!"

I wanted to see and hear more, but then they cut to a diaper commercial. While young moms were beaming at their babies, I was escorted through a little-used door and out on the tarmac, where a military-type vehicle was waiting. We drove for a long time, nobody saying any-thing. Finally, we stopped in front of a Walgreens and another man joined us. This man seemed vaguely Middle-Eastern. He started speaking to me in another language, as if he expected me to speak it too.

"Is that Arabic? Are you speaking to me in Arabic?" I asked.

The man stopped talking. There was a long pause.

"If it is Arabic, then I don't know what you just said. If it isn't, I don't speak that language either."

He stared at me some more. Then he said in English, "We've got as much time as you do."

I shrugged. He shrugged back. We drove on in silence. The man to my right continued silently chewing gum. In all the hours we drove, I never saw him remove the piece he was chewing, nor add another one.

MEMO
Surrounded by Assholes

From: Richard M. Nixon

To: Henry Kissinger

Henry, you above all should know that I have little tolerance for ass-kissers, wimps of any kind, and assholes who think they are anything but. So, if this fellow you have been tracking seems to not belong in those leagues, then I concur, bring him to us. Let's get to know a soul brother, a like-minded patriot.

Why didn't you respond to my last memo? I urged you to hop on this and you never responded. You think it's easy for me to type these memos? My jowls drape onto the keyboard. After Rosemary Woods betrayed me, I won't dictate anything to anybody. You think you're better than me Mr. Nobel Peace Prize? They considered giving Hitler one of those. You get the Nobel and I get booted out of office. No, I'm not dictating any memos.

How difficult it is nowadays to find someone who is not working for the Jews or the Communists. Sometimes I look around myself in Washington and I think I am in a synagogue, or have somehow stumbled into the Kremlin itself. I'm well aware that you're a Hebe, but you're not a practicing Yid.

When the Papist or the Jew sees an opportunity to delude someone less conniving or crafty, he takes full advantage. Kennedy, friend to the Negro! Don't make me laugh. We need men who are not soft inside, who cannot be brought by cheap sympathy to do the bidding of our enemies. Hoover knows what I'm talking about here. As do you, Henry. If he is such a man, let's bring him into the fold as quickly as we can.

21

Have Hoover check to see if he's a faggot. We don't need any more of them on our team. Hoover should have no trouble seeing who's light in the loafers, for it takes one to know one. Dammit, Henry, let's get this Glass Eater on board!

3. Paraguay

When we came to a clearing in a dense woods, it was already dark, but I could tell that it was some sort of air strip. And sure enough, there was an airplane waiting for us, a military plane. The seats faced backwards. The three of us were the only passengers. By this time, I had decided not to speak unless spoken to, and since no one was talking, I had no idea of our destination. I did know we had been aloft for many hours before landing at an airstrip in the middle of a forest. Had we simply flown in circles all that time? No, here the vegetation was different, the sounds of birds unfamiliar. Now it was morning, maybe a few hours past dawn. From there we drove a while in another vehicle, this time a Mercedes-Benz limo. Finally, we arrived at what seemed to be a hotel, built in the style of an alpine chalet.

I had slept on the plane, but not well, and so I was a bit groggy by the time we entered the building. The first people I saw looked strangely familiar. Then I realized who they were. George W. Bush, Donald Rumsfeld and Dick Cheney were hanging out near the bar at one end of a large dining room. In the middle of the room, near the head of a long dining room table, slumped in a wheelchair and not talking to anyone, was Richard Nixon. Though my brain clouded, I did some quick figuring and estimated that he must be over a hundred. He looked every day of it. But here he was alive! And for some reason, someone had gone to great lengths to bring me to him!

23

Hillary Clinton and Condoleezza Rice entered the room dressed in tennis clothes and holding rackets. They looked in my direction and nodded to my two escorts, who quickly left the room. Condy came up to me.

"How was your flight?" she asked.

"No peanuts, no drinks, but at least we didn't crash," I answered.

Hillary seemed to find my response hilarious, because she snorted, and soon the others followed. Within seconds even Nixon smiled, though he might have simply been suffering from gas.

"I can eat an ashtray if anybody would like to wager," I said.

Nobody said anything for a while. Nixon began to drool from the corner of his jowls.

Condy came in closer. "You want to eat an ashtray?"

"A glass one. It's what I do. You bet that I can't, and I do it anyway."

"How big an ashtray?" Rumsfeld asked.

"Anything you got."

There was some discussion among different groups in the room. Finally, Cheney snapped his fingers and a waiter came to me, carrying a large, glass ashtray.

"I'll need a hammer and a sock," I added. Someone translated my request into Spanish. The waiter returned with a rusty hammer and an old blue sock after a few minutes.

"By the way, where are we?" I asked Hillary.

She responded, "Paraguay."

It was all making sense now. I remembered the Bush family had purchased a large estate in Paraguay just before he left office.

As I began the process of reducing the ashtray to shards, another man in a wheelchair entered the room. It was Henry Kissinger, and he pulled up, parking himself next to Nixon.

"I'll wager ten thousand dollars that he can," Rumsfeld announced.

Cheney piped in, "Five thousand that he can't."

"I'll match that," Hillary piped in.

Nixon started mumbling and then said very clearly "I'll suck Kissinger's cock if he can."

The room erupted in laughter. Kissinger mimed unzipping himself and the crowd roared again.

Then some men in colorful shirts carrying harps and over-sized guitars entered the room and began singing what I assume was Paraguayan music. We were in for the long haul. The party was just beginning. I wondered if this were the South American version of San Francisco's Bohemian Grove gatherings.

It took me six hours to eat such a large ashtray, and by the time I finished many of my hosts had already lost interest and drifted away, but Hillary and Condy stayed with me to the end. When I had a moment alone with Hillary, I whispered, "I thought you were on the other side."

"I stick with the winners," she whispered back.

Suddenly the party was over, at least for me. A couple of men in dark suits approached, one holding a black hood, which he put over my head. From there I was escorted out of the dining room and into another room, which might have been as big as the first, but since there was little sound, I couldn't tell. From there I was made to crouch and enter a smaller room, except that acoustically it felt a lot like the same room. Then they took off the hood and I could see that I was inside a cage in the middle of another ballroom or dining room, only this one was dimly lit. This was to be my home for the next five days.

My escorts turned out the lights as soon as my cage door was locked, and the only illumination came from an exit sign on the other side of the room. They had provided a mat, and I quickly fell asleep, awakening to a ballroom full of sunlight pouring in through the tall windows.

My first visitors were a Boy Scout troupe. They were respectful and silent as they gathered around, whispering among each other until their leader told them I was a recently-apprehended terrorist and that there was a ten million-dollar bounty on my head. Then the whispering stopped and they simply stared. I smiled. Then I growled and they became rigid and quiet. They all had cameras on their cellphones and snapped away as they backed away from me.

A Girl Scout Troop came next, but they kept much more distance than the boys, and many of them refused to look at me at all, feigning interest instead in the windows and furniture of the room itself. After they left, I was served lunch, which I wolfed down. Then Condy came to see me.

"We want to thank you for your cooperation. Our campaign needed a victory and even though we know this is all entirely invented, well, so was our invasion of Iraq. Fabrication is an important executive function. A fully-functioning democracy is a difficult myth to maintain, and having you here is helping keep it afloat," she said.

"I don't remember agreeing to anything," I said.

"It was tacit. There will be a simulated execution in a few days. Then you'll be handsomely rewarded and relocated. What's your feeling about Indiana?"

"Don't know much about it. I was born there, but we moved to Chicago when I was still a toddler."

"We know that. Peru, Indiana is interested in helping us with this. Real estate is a real bargain in Peru. Not a bad place, either. Noel Coward was from Peru. It's everything wrong and right about small town America."

"Isn't it easier to hide in a big city?"

"That's what they say, but if you move to a place like Peru, Indiana, everybody's glad to see you. As long as you make a good first impression, you're golden. If you tell them you're a nudist or an atheist or that you believe homosexuals should marry, then we'll just have to relocate you again."

"Lightning bugs on a summer night. Listening to the ball game on the radio."

"Beats Gitmo any day."

"But why me in the first place?"

"You made the mistake of pissing off your wife. She's a well-connected woman with some strong opinions of her own, especially about you. When she made up her mind, it was set in stone. Fortunately, her offer to us came at a time when we could use an unconventional scapegoat such as yourself. One with no support network to speak of. Few close friends. A guy like you can disappear and cause nary a ripple."

I saw her point. Instead of gaining a sort of freedom from not cultivating ties, I had become an invisible, forgotten man. Not the kind of guy you need to torture or repress, because I wasn't trying to do much of anything at all. I was a thorn in no one's side; instead I was a shadow creeping along the wall. My lack of zest had put me in the position to be the perfect fall guy. A puppet without a puppet master.

Well this puppet was determined to find some way to break his strings, or at least tangle them. I had to lay low and wait for opportunity. Despite her assurances otherwise, would I be executed in a few days? Probably not, but who knows what other lies Condy could tell with a straight face? She and her cronies had a lot of experience in that area.

My thoughts were interrupted by someone flipping a switch and the curtains pulling aside to reveal a large TV screen. A shrill soundtrack echoed through the ballroom. It was deafening. The images looked vaguely familiar. And then I realized what I was watching.

They were showing me my favorite kids show from the fifties, Andy's Gang. There was Andy, the inept host, ill-kempt and in ill health. He kept trying to say something but Froggy kept interrupting him. Sixty years

27

later I still found the character of Froggy to be terrifying. And Andy Devine was hideous. I kept waiting for him to clear his throat, but he only grew hoarser over time. The show was so mind-numbingly stupid that even at the age of five I must have known something was deeply wrong here. When they had nothing to show they cut back to a stock shot of the kids in the audience laughing dementedly. Froggy would use his magic powers for evil to confuse Andy (no difficult task) and make him do what he never intended.

Yes, Cheney and Rumsfeld had done their research well. How many of our tax dollars had gone into determining which television shows their future torture victims had watched as children?

M E M O
Fight the Good Fight

From: J. Edgar Hoover
To: Richard M. Nixon, Henry Kissinger

Gentlemen: I am still surprised and delighted every day I realize that we have successfully kept our longevity a secret. If you had told me that using the organs of a few unfortunates would allow the leaders of our great society to not only survive, but stay active and continue the struggle, I would not have believed you. "Science Fiction," I would have said. But now I realize that all great work has always been done in secret, and that those who have incorporated the rigors of secrecy into the core of our beings should never apologize for our work mode.

Even though Rumsfeld and Cheney are still out there in the public eye, doing what they can to take the heat for W, we are much more effective behind the scenes. This Glass Eater may indeed prove to be an asset, but even if he fails to conform, we are bound to succeed in the long run. Let the niggers riot. It's what they do best. Crowd control is now a science. Ferguson proved our abilities in that area. The Patriot Act is permanently enshrined in our very Constitution. The Average American is waiting patiently for subliminal instruction. We have already won whatever it was we were fighting for.

Nothing in his profile suggests that this Glass Eater is a faggot, but that doesn't mean he isn't one. Nowadays, nobody seems to care much either way, but I know Dick still holds the line on buggery.

29

4. Getting Info the Hard Way

The television torture went on for eight hours or so. Every once in a while, a nurse with a clipboard would quietly enter the room and record my reactions. At first I waved at her and smiled, but later on I ignored her. The last few times I must have been asleep, though my sleep was fitful, as every time Froggy laughed his horrible laugh I convulsed.

The next morning I awoke to find a beautiful young woman was staring at me. She was dressed in a brightly colored polyester uniform, the kind favored by fast food employees.

"A broken old man with shattered dreams," she cooed. "We get a lot of those. Do you want breakfast?"

"Pancakes," I replied. "I was dreaming about pancakes."

"This is your lucky day!" she assured me. "Smothered in imitation maple syrup, with a side of greasy sausage links, just the way you like 'em."

Unfortunately, she brought me no pancakes, but instead, continued to tease and make fun of me the rest of the morning. Then a man brought me a Burger King Double Whopper Combo Meal with bacon, large fries and a chocolate shake. It amazed me that such a thing could be found in Paraguay, but I inhaled it and felt just as bad as I usually do afterwards. It was nauseatingly comforting in a nostalgic way.

31

As I sat there burping and swishing the grease around in my mouth, another couple of men came and handed me a swimming suit, which they indicated I should put on. I did, and then we sat in the back of an open jeep and drove a short way to a river, where they motioned that I should enter the water and swim. This I did as well. The water was a pleasant temperature, not terribly clear, but not filthy. It smelled ok. I decided to swim downstream and made rapid progress. When I turned around after a few minutes, the men were gone. I was swimming through farmland. A herd of cows grazed a mile or so up on a hillside. I was enjoying myself at last!

Rounding a bend, I saw a large group of what looked like girl high school students in the traditional high school uniform—jumper, knee socks, white shirts with peter pan collar—jumping up and down in unison. Through a bullhorn, a woman was barking orders at them in Spanish. I waved, but no one seemed to notice me.

Then the bends came more quickly, the river narrowed and the current picked up. I was going quite fast, and that's when I saw the fish leaping from the water. Little fish with big teeth. Very big teeth. Teeth so sharp that I didn't feel the bites at first. They started with my toes, then my knees, and finally my elbows and hands. By the time I pulled myself up on the bank, it looked like somebody had poured a bucket of red paint on me.

I tried sitting on some stones and strategically dipping parts of me back into the water to wash off the blood, but that just infuriated the fish all the more, and many of them leaped up onto the rocks and grass, lying on their sides, opening and closing their jaws in one last attempt to get me. That's when I noticed I was being shot at.

The bullets arrived before the crack of the rifles. They had the power to break off chips of rock, while some merely slapped the sand and mud on the river bank. I looked up the hill and saw a party of five shooting at me. It was Hillary, Condy, Don, Dick and a black man in an army uniform who I took to be Colin Powell. I reasoned that he would probably be the best shot of the bunch, so I kept a close eye on him as I ran into some nearby bushes. I could hear laughter and whoops of encouragement as they took turns trying to kill me.

Walking on the sharp stones, my feet were unhappy, as was the rest of me. If they really wanted to kill me, surely there were easier ways of accomplishing it. So, what was this about? I didn't have time to really think it through, for they continued to shoot randomly at the bushes, so I decided it would be best to back up while keeping as low to the ground as possible. That's when I noticed the video cameras in the nearby trees.

Thus began my long and remunerative career in entertainment. It turned out this whole episode was being taped for a new show that became a world-wide hit overnight. *Bad Boys Pay the Price*, a new type of crime/game show comedy that filled a niche nobody knew was there, but once it was born it inspired many a competitor. As soon as I stumbled back to the hotel, scratched and bruised, I was hailed as a hero. The penthouse suite. Complimentary room service, massage by a lovely young woman. The next morning, they flew me first class back to the States and gave me enough money to rent a deluxe condo in LA.

The whole experience had been some sort of audition, and I won the role. I became the star of the season opener, and was asked to reprise my role many times, though at the advice of my agent I demurred, holding out for film work. Some of us only have one shot at the top, and we have to maximize our advantages when they appear.

Turns out everyone, even politico heavyweights, wants to be in show biz. The lure of being a movie star is always beckoning those who have tasted the first kiss of celebrity. In fact, the whole Bush inner circle have been pitching screenplay concepts for years, and for some reason I was the one who unwittingly carried the ball into the end zone. They had already set up a film studio in Capital Miranda, just up the road from Encarnación, using the German-styled Hotel Tyrol as headquarters. Dr. Josef Mengele had lived there, as had many other Nazis. The long-time dictator of Paraguay had used it as a place to entertain high school girls his henchmen would collect for his pleasure. Now we were cranking out a TV series, sometimes using crew and talent from neighboring Argentina. Posadas, Argentina was right across the Parana river, and the that country enjoyed a thriving film industry. The difference in personality and demeanor of the people from these two countries separated by a half mile of water couldn't have been more different. I enjoyed them both, for different reasons.

After we wrapped the TV series and an action movie where most of the filming would take place elsewhere and later, I decided to treat myself to a vacation and went as far south as I could go, to Patagonia, which was a lot like Norway or Alaska. Prices were triple what I was used to paying up north, but that's ok, I was rich now and on my way to becoming even richer. In Bariloche, I met an old man who swore to me that Hitler had lived there for many years, after arriving on submarine in the last days of the war.

I found it lonely traveling as a rich person. Everyone I met was very nice, solicitous, but that didn't buy me a sense of belonging. Sometimes the loneliness was painful, especially when I'd see something really lovely and have no one to whom I could say, "Will you look at that?"

So, I moved back to America, to Hot Springs, Arkansas, a place I'd always thought I might enjoy. I was wrong. It was a bore.

A few weeks later, I met a taxi driver who told me that he had a screenplay "concept" that he wanted to pitch me. I guess he recognized me when I got in his cab. His story idea involved Scarlett Johansson and I as a couple of witty, cynical detectives. Kind of an updated version of the *Thin Man*. I said it sounded promising and told him to contact my agent. Suddenly he became crestfallen.

"You're blowing me off. Nick Cage had the same reaction when I pitched him Lethal Injection Four. He pretended to be interested, but when I called his agent they'd never heard of me or my concept. You guys get big and you forget what it's like for us little guys. It's hell, that's what it is. Living hell."

I felt bad, but what could I do? People were suddenly coming at me in waves, each wanting something. There was only one of me, but there were thousands, maybe millions of them.

MEMO
Victory is Ours

From: Condoleezza Rice

To: The Boys Club

When I read the papers, or find myself talking to someone I have just met, I am amazed by the level of ignorance that persists even among the educated. Nobody knows what's really going on, and that's the way we like it, right? Putting aside the fact that almost no one really wants to know what is really going on, it is a statement of our efficacy that such a simple notion as national security could be expanded to achieve such a broad spectrum of concerns. This making the world safe for democracy has served us well and shows no signs of flagging. No one seems to mind that the War on Terror imagines an enemy as amorphous as a fog bank.

It's fun to be able to achieve our goals without the hindrance of asking nincompoops for their opinion. Democracy is a tedious process, which is why anyone who's really striving to make something happen tries to avoid it if at all possible.

And let's not forget to give credit where it is due. "They hate us for our freedoms," was a work of genius. The runt of the litter made us all proud that day.

Again, good work boys. Hillary and I will do what we can to cheer you on.

5. Reunited

A few days later, I got word that my wife was trying to contact me. Apparently, she was under the impression that she deserved some sort of finder's fee for launching my career. A Judas-agent fee. I told my handlers I wasn't interested in communicating with her, but she persisted and finally showed up at my front door about dawn one morning.

"What a dump!" she said, and before I could react she strode right past me.

"Are you alone?"

"Natasha, what a surprise," I blustered. "Coffee?"

"You realize you've started a glass eating craze across America. Children are dying."

"Always nice to see you. What brings you this far?"

"But now you're Mr. Big Shot. Move over Vin Diesel and The Rock! Couldn't have happened to a nicer guy. Couldn't have happened without my help. Kissinger and Nixon are crazy about you. They still wield a lot of influence, especially among old, white men, who still really run everything even if they pretend to have shared some power with women and a few token minorities."

"Yes, good people, all."

Have I ever told you how much I despise the lot of you?"

I contemplated a witty reply, but concluded there would be no fun in playing this game. "Yes, many times," I answered. We sat in silence. I waited for her

39

to broach the subject of why she was here. I suppose she was waiting for me to be the first to ask. The way I see it, if you barge into someone's apartment at six in the morning, you're the one who ought to do the talking.

"All right, I want you to take me back. I made a terrible mistake. I was so unhappy, and even though it wasn't your fault, I wanted to make you suffer as much as I suffered. Please forgive me Ronald...I mean, Donald. Please, let's try to be happy again."

I didn't say anything for a while. I tried to remember when we were happy together. Try as I might, it didn't come. Then I thought about the name slip-up, and wondered how many men she was seeing.

"I never got the impression that you actually liked me," I told her.

"I didn't, but that was my fault, not yours. You're a perfectly likeable person. It's obvious. It's always been obvious, only I couldn't see it until now."

"But what about your drinking problem?"

"I'm planning to quit any day now. I'm already in therapy. They've told me I'm not a bad person, just a sick person getting better. I've already halved my vodka intake. I feel better than I have in years!"

I had to admit she looked good. But I was afraid that without her zany side, there wouldn't be much to her. I didn't say that; I just thought it. The zany side had definitely worn out its welcome, and there was no guarantee there existed another side that would make us compatible.

"Let me think about it," I offered. She frowned. I have learned that those who would not grant you the time to make a considered decision do not have your best interests at heart.

"You'll never forgive me. I can't say I blame you, but I want you to know that you're killing me. Your resentment is like a dagger pointed at my heart."

With that she put both hands over her left breast and sighed. I felt I was watching a silent movie heroine in action. So now it all boiled down to being my fault. She who had turned me over to the authorities was playing the victim and the choice to make this all better was strictly mine.

"You're the one who should be the TV star, not me," I told her.

"You're right, of course. There's no justice in this world," she sighed.

We agreed to a trial reconciliation, the terms of which would be re-negotiated after two weeks. It was all sweetness and light at first. She was overly solicitous, serving me coffee in bed the moment I awoke. Then I entered our bedroom one afternoon and found her on a Skype call with Kissinger, and could hear Nixon mumbling and grunting in assent, though he was off-camera. She was also using a Ouija board, which I thought was unusual.

"I didn't know you were into that," I commented as blandly as possible.

"Just something to pass the time," she replied.

"Wasn't that Henry Kissinger you were talking to?"

"Yes. He asked about you. How's that glass eating husband of yours?"

"I'm a movie star now. Glass eating is a thing of the past. Like furnace repair."

"You can leave the ashtrays alone now? This I have to see."

"Yes."

"But you can't leave me alone, can you? No, I'm like an addiction. An all-consuming addiction."

"Have you been drinking?"

"Just a little. It helps take the edge off. Oh please, don't be a scold. It's so un-sexy."

41

"I don't have an opinion about whether you should drink or not. I just know that I don't enjoy being around it."

"That's what you say, but you know it's not true. You know you want me, drunk or sober. You're just using my drinking as an excuse to protect yourself from being vulnerable. You're afraid of not getting what you want, what you need, what you're addicted to."

With that she left the Ouija board behind and came towards me. I resisted the impulse to run out the door, and instead embraced her. She smelled like vodka and cigarettes, not my favorite scent.

Even though it felt like I was trapped in a 1940s-melodrama starring Victor Mature and Loretta Young, I kept on with her, vowing every night that I would tell her the next morning how I really felt, but by then I had lost my resolve and had to accumulate a new batch of resolve in the face of the accumulated evidence of that day. Sudden mood swings, hysterical laughter one moment and tears the next. I remembered what it had been like dating less volatile women before I met Natasha, and I must confess I found them predictable and a bit boring, though surely more comforting than any time spent with my Russian doll.

Meanwhile, the offers kept pouring in for acting work, but most of them were absurdly inappropriate. I was offered roles that more prominent actors had already rejected in vehicles that seemed doomed from the outset. Lex Luther in Superman 15, Willy Loman in a hip-hop version of Death of a Salesman. Someone who should have known better wanted me to play Helen Keller's father in a sentimental Hallmark Family Special. I felt a kinship with Nicholas Cage and Liam Neeson, who seemed to lack the gumption to say No! to a doomed project.

To each of these, I instructed my handlers to issue a polite yet firm, 'Thanks but not today. Please keep me in mind, though." I didn't want to risk burning any bridges at this stage in my career, but I hoped that someone in a position of power would finally be able to see the real me, and the real scope of my talent, before senility set in. If any of this was an indication of what I could expect from my show biz career, I might want to go back to faux furnace repair.

I began to wonder if Natasha and I would have an easier time of holding our marriage together if only we shared a mutual career. Maybe I could get a TV series launched for the two of us. Surely some of the tried and true TV formulas of the past would work for us. Maybe a modern update of the Billy Jack movies of the seventies ... righteous hippy couple fights the squares. Combine that with cute young cops, sarcastic medical students, and a few cute kids or pets, and someone with a longer attention span than mine might create a recipe for a long-running hit that would bond Natasha and I together, along with plenty of cash. Didn't I owe us one last whole-hearted shot at marital and financial success?

I remembered a terrible summer replacement series starring Peggy Cass and Jack Weston as parents of a family of diaper-clad chimpanzees. I even remembered the name, *The Hathaways*. Why can I remember this drek and not my phone number?

It turned out it wasn't up to me. I guess I shouldn't be surprised that my former captors had a scheme in mind that was far beyond my ability to imagine the many twists and turns. When Kim Jong-Un came to our front door, I figured he was an impersonator, and this had to be some sort of Hollywood prank, sort of like having Elvis sing you happy birthday or finding Marilyn Monroe in your bed.

But it really was the infamous North Korean dictator, and he really was there to see me. Through his translator, he told me that Dennis Rodman had recommended me for a feature length film about Karaoke-singing volleyball stars who take gold at the Olympics while becoming International Entertainment Sensations. I would play the promoter who never loses faith in them no matter what obstacles cross their path, including a preemptive nuclear strike by the United States, whose women's volleyball team failed to qualify for the finals. I told him the concept sounded original and interesting, but I'd have to check my schedule.

Finally, there was a bidding war. Various firms were offering me larger and larger amounts of money not to sign with another firm. This was called "an exclusive option on my services," though the exact nature of those services was left up in the air. They were simply bidding for me to sign with them and no one else. My agent assured me that in most cases nothing real ever comes from these options, but the money would prove real, and substantial.

I had discovered a legitimate way to provide no real service or benefit to anyone and still be handsomely rewarded for my lack of effort. The Capitalist's Dream! Having stumbled upon it, you might think I would finally be content, but instead I was growing more dissatisfied by the minute. How dare these people patronize me this way! Didn't I have my newly reclaimed sense of high self-esteem bordering on pride?

If not proud, I was certainly lonely. I missed the personal touch, the one-on-one contact I enjoyed back when I was swindling old ladies in their living rooms and basements. Now, money came to me anonymously, through the machinations of my agent and the largesse of creative directors at entertainment studios. I didn't feel like any of it had much to do with me.

Money makes some things easier. Problems disappear in the face of ample funds. Of course, there are numerous opportunities to use money to manufacture new problems, and I seem especially adept at that process. It's another one of my many counter-productive talents.

MEMO
Glass Eater

From: Donald Rumsfeld
To: Central American Operations Team

For our purposes, we will refer to this individual as GLASSEATER, for reasons that should be obvious. He has been sighted in both Honduras and Nicaragua. His latest knows location is Ometepe Island, Nicaragua. Why a man of his means travels in Third World shit holes is still unknown, and the only company he keeps seems to be people he meets for the first time on his journeys. He appears to wander.

For reasons that should surprise no one, Nicaragua is no friend of the United States, and although there seems to be no political motive to his travel there, it is not inconceivable that he may approach or be approached by leftists, Sandinistas, or their agents. His current apolitical stance may be a ruse or not. Time will tell.

One person with whom he has been in contact is well known to us, a Mr. Paul Douglas of Minneapolis, a man who considers himself to be Jesus reincarnated. Mr. Douglas has been a long-time resident of Honduras, El Salvador and Nicaragua, and although he enters these countries on simple tourist visas, he has never come to the attention of the border patrols or immigration control in any of these countries. My guess he simply flies under the radar. His scruffy appearance does not invite scrutiny, as he would be an unlikely candidate from whom to extract a bribe.

Again, at this point we have no reason to believe his contact with Mr. Douglas is anything more than a casual acquaintance. Douglas was once hospitalized for psychiatric reasons in the 1970's but at least in his home country has not been hospitalized since.

45

One other item of note: the GLASSEATER'S ex-wife Natasha is romantically involved with our own Dick Cheney. Despite Dick's notorious proclivity for sexual dalliance with anyone and everyone, age and appearance notwithstanding, we think this a curious fact, and strain to chalk it up to coincidence. Again, time will tell, but our boys back at the NSA are doing their best to find out.

6. Peru

The move to Peru, Indiana was uneventful. Since I owned almost nothing, I was able to make the trip with just one extra suitcase. Natasha said she would come later, that she had something to take care of, but I knew in my heart that she wouldn't be joining me, which was fine. Her duplicity saved me from having to summon the spine to tell her I wanted to be free.

So, I decided to start a school, an entrepreneurial academy to teach Leadership! That was the hot thing, Leadership! that and Passion, with a capital **P**. Everyone was gaga over Leadership and Passion, and I wasn't about to stand by and let others take the credit or the lion's share of the booty. Creativity was also quite sexy at the time, and I promised to unblock and unleash it in every student. After all, I was a certified success, wasn't I? Surely there was an easy and direct path for someone of my stature to help others achieve even a modicum of what I had.

Peru, Indiana turned out to be the perfect place to establish such an academy. I could lease an enormous commercial building for almost nothing, as half of downtown had been abandoned once Wal-Mart established itself on the edge of town. I settled on an old Elks Club. The furnishings that had been left behind were massive, grandiose, and free for the taking. These lent an air of legitimacy to my latest whim.

Hiring faculty was no problem, either. Over the years, I had surrounded myself with a plethora of the over-educated and the under-employed. Men and women who had last showed promise—so long ago that no one could quite recall what those promises were—now sent in their resumes. Braggarts, dullards, nincompoops, poseurs. No matter, today they would be more than willing to work for slightly above minimum wage, just to have a private office with their name on the door, preceded by the title *Professor*.

There is no scam like education, for the marks line up and take out loans just to participate. You assign readings and then after a suitable amount of "discussion," test them on the readings. You don't even have to write the assigned readings, in fact, it's better if you don't. That way you risk nothing!

Education is the only scam where the mark continues to credit and thank his tormentor long after he should have realized he'd been taken for a ride. As my celebrity status increased, the fortunes of my academy soared. There was interest in me giving a TED talk. I demurred, citing a busy schedule. I encouraged my staff to organize symposia, and they did, charging outlandish fees for other no-talents to come and give talks about their derivative "research" to an equally mediocre audience.

Then I went a bit too far. I decided that it was time to bring in some heavyweights. When I invited Henry Kissinger to receive an honorary Doctorate in Leadership! I knew I was treading on thin ice. This could easily blow up in my face, but the temptation was simply too strong to resist. After all, hadn't he received the Nobel Peace Prize after bombing Laos back into the stone age? What could be so wrong about receiving an honorary doctorate from a diploma mill like mine?

It turns out the CIA had their own opinion about my offer. Suddenly, our little campus was crawling with creeps, athletic young men and women who looked like they had already endured plenty of special training, and I'm not talking about poetry class.

Finally, they confronted me in my office, having determined with substantial evidence that my academy

48

was a fraud, my faculty a group of dullards, and that nothing of value was being taught or learned.

"And your point ... is?" I countered.

It was a brilliant day in early autumn. The maple trees on the front lawn were aflame. Little did I realize that the main building and our new annex would soon be aflame as well, and that although no one lost their life in the mysterious blaze, the institution I had founded only months before would soon be no more than a hazy memory, an incomplete transcript.

Thank God I'd had the foresight to include "No Refunds" in the terms and conditions for admission. I owed the lawyer who suggested that golden tidbit a lot. Maybe I'll award him an honorary doctorate someday.

I thought maybe this would be an excellent time to take the North Korean dictator up on his generous offer, but by then he had changed his mind and was more impressed with persuading Justin Bieber to become his new Minister of Culture.

So, I was back to Square One. For someone who had just been wiped out, I was remarkably at ease, for I had not owned much of what was lost. In fact, I'm sure with a little digging I could find some sort of government handout for business owners who had suffered a catastrophic fire. Even an interest-free loan might suffice. No, I was not sitting in the hot seat, but I was straddling a fence, as I had no idea what to do next. All I knew for sure was the discomfort of fence-sitting.

I thought briefly about starting a religion, but then surmised that would be too much like my recent foray into higher education. Taking advantage of the irrational beliefs of others is child's play. Surely someone as clever as I could come up with a scam more novel, one that required more original thought and would be a bit harder to decipher.

That's when I came up with the Psychic Bypass. As long as I didn't make the mistake of predicting exactly where on the heart these new arteries would grow, or when, there was indisputable evidence that one could

49

increase blood flow to damaged heart muscle simply by staying alive long enough for it to happen. Survival could be insured by taking conventional medications to control blood pressure and to inhibit coagulation, but who could seriously dispute the fact that attitude and prudent exercise couldn't share the credit for a new blood supply? The burden of proof lay on the scoffer.

The trick of making claims while not legally making them has been well-studied. What with tens of millions of baby-boomers reaching heart attack age, Psychic Bypass was a guaranteed winner. But then, after I had lined up scores of interviews on health and fitness shows, and had what seemed real interest on a segment of the Lifetime cable channel, when Facebook and Twitter were ready to go viral with an explosion of Psychic Bypass *likes, shares* and *tweets,* when it came time to launch, I did what I always do. I got bored.

I found myself asking, "Do I really want to spend these last chapters of my life fooling others into wasting their dwindling hours? No. Surely there is something more fun to be done."

What I would really enjoy is out there, just over the next horizon, and all I have to do is wait a bit longer for it to rise.

Contemplation, Patience ... these reared their awful heads and demanded my attention. Before they had had their way with me, during the forty to forty-five seconds I dared examine my heretofore unexamined life, I thought I would not be able to draw another breath. Nausea came in waves. But as they left, the certainty arrived that, Yes, I would survive. I am me, dammit, and that just has to be good enough. Sure, I'm a sociopath of sorts, but what of it? I'm not alone. Many whom we grant positions of prominence share my proclivity.

I've always enjoyed reading the stories of other people who greatly changed their lives halfway through. Dr. Albert Schweitzer, Mother Theresa, Edgar Buchanan, who played Uncle Joe on *Petticoat Junction,* one of many forgettable TV shows from the seventies.

But he was unforgettable, because he was a character actor with real character. A former dentist, he only became an actor at the age of thirty-six. He's best known as Uncle Joe, a role he played across three different television shows—*Petticoat Junction, Green Acres* and *The Beverly Hillbillies.* One could say he owned the role of Uncle Joe.

Yes, Edgar Buchanan gave me hope. He was completely self-invented, absolutely authentic, and people appreciated him for who he was. He wasn't John Barrymore. He was a dentist from Oregon who moved to Hollywood in mid-life to become an actor, a move that changed not only his life but the lives of millions. Forever.

It seems my hankering for ultimate significance and my boredom and revulsion with life as I had been living it was responsible for the germination of a new idea. I could really be of service. No more scams.

Such an idea had never before occurred to me because I never thought it would be possible for me to do anything without a hidden motive or agenda. My very nature was duplicitous. I had accepted duplicity as a given. But maybe being an imposter was simply a role I had chosen to play, and anytime I chose to play another role, I could let the false one drop.

So began yet another chapter in my life. Suddenly I was Joe Lunchbucket, except without a job to define him. I was nobody in particular, certainly nobody special. On the other hand, I was keeping a low profile, so in all probability I had nothing to fear. I still had more money than I knew what to do with.

The only job I could find without misrepresenting myself was that of Wal-Mart Greeter. Apparently, there's a high turnover, as some folks find it too stressful. I found it suited my personality and proclivities rather well. I could space out and do very little—if that's what I felt like—just handing people shopping carts; or if I felt talkative, if there was fire in my gut that needed expression, I could pour on the charm.

51

"How are you folks tonight?"

"My that's a nice dress!"

"The family that shops together stays together."

Sometimes things got quite slow at Wal-Mart. Nobody wanted my greetings or my help with a cart. At those times, I was able to dream up Meaningless Inspirational Slogans, much like the ones we had sent to teenage models as cell phone affirmations. Here I was thinking of placards, posters, framed statements to hang in board rooms to show a commitment to excellence. Eagles, sunsets over the ocean, proud stags lifting their mighty antlers aloft.

"Be Everything!"

"Never Apologize, Instead Inspire!"

"Excuses are like jelly beans, one is too many and a thousand aren't enough."

"Wings and Imaginations Need to be Stretched to Fly!!"

I would write these down in a little notebook I carried in my blue Wal-Mart greeter vest, the one that said "Sam" (my *nom du Wal-Mart*) on the pocket. After a few weeks, I made the mistake of showing them to the Assistant Manager.

"These are great!" he exclaimed. "Let me show them to the Manager. I knew you weren't just a Greeter."

The next week they asked if I could make a presentation at a management training seminar to be held in a nearby hotel. They assured me I'd still be on the clock even if I was off-site. I agreed.

Well, wouldn't you know it but Sam Walton's son just happened to be at that seminar, and he was so impressed he asked if he could license my slogans and print them for in-house use. I agreed to that, as well, and then within a month the plan had changed to embossing them on laminated plaques and selling them at every Wal-Mart in the English-speaking world, with plans to translate them into thirty-two other languages.

That's when Natasha came back into my life. She and Dick Cheney had checked into a motel just blocks from my house in Peru, Indiana, after registering as "Mr. and Mrs. Donald Rumsfeld." I had no inkling that they were a couple, but once I realized it, the idea seemed as grotesque as it was inevitable.

She called just as I was leaving for my morning stroll around the neighborhood, what people used to call a constitutional. She asked if they could come over. I asked, "Who's we?" and that's when she broke the news about her being hooked up with the former VP and Halliburton CEO.

I told them I would be back in forty-five minutes, "Make it an hour," and I would be glad to serve them instant coffee and what was left of a box of Oreos. When I got back home there were four SUV's parked in front of my house, each with tinted windows. I could dimly make out men sitting inside wearing sunglasses. As I approached my front door, I heard the SUV door locks snap open, sounding *en masse* like the rifles of a firing squad being cocked at once.

After I opened the door, five men wearing earpieces pushed past me and quickly went through each room in house. In less than a minute they reappeared, returning to their vehicles. Then Natasha and Cheney emerged, deep in conversation, seemingly oblivious to my presence. I stood at the door and waved them inside, Cheney giving me his trademark smirk as he passed.

I broke out the Nescafe and the Oreos (both, by the way, products of Nestlé®, a Swiss corporation with major holdings in Halliburton.) We exchanged pleasantries. Then Cheney got down to business.

"I suppose you're wondering why we're here. Why are your ex-wife and I, two of the most reviled people the planet, sitting in your living room? Well, I'll tell you why. We want you to stand up to the enemy. We want you to risk taking a bullet for your country. Fact is, you're not afraid to be an asshole and neither am I, and that's the kind of people America needs right now."

I couldn't really follow him, but I nodded in assent so he would keep talking.

"I know I'm one of the most despised men in America. I planned it that way. Being popular is for wimps. I can take the heat, and believe me, somebody has to in order to get anything done. Oil is not a luxury, it's a necessity. He who has access to oil is powerful and secure. Those who don't are just hanging on by a thread, even if they're not aware of it. The world, especially America, is full of new-age wimps, liberal arts graduates who think solar energy is going to solve all their problems. Solar isn't going to solve shit, and least not while any of us are alive. So, the question is, do we want to live in a Third World shit hole and buy our gasoline from people who might suddenly decide not to sell it to us, or do we want to be in charge of our own destiny? What do you want?"

"I want to be left alone."

"That's what you think and say, but it's not true. You want to be taken care of, just like everybody else. You depend on infrastructure and services that you've come to take for granted. When they're suddenly not there, you freak out and demand an explanation. You're a normal American."

"So, what can I do for my country?"

"You can stop lying to yourself and others. You can man up to the fact that it's them or us."

"Who's them?"

"Who isn't? Do you think we have allies? Friends? When the shit hits the fan, everybody is going to duck at the same time. Your wife has bigger balls than you do, but she lacks your talent for deception. You're a real sleaze ball. You're perfect for this kind of work.

We want you to spend a few months in Viet Nam, starting up a phony Internet business. Then we want you to move to North Korea and become buddies with the fat guy. Eventually, we want you to wind up in Iran helping them advise North Korea on nuclear reactors and weapons manufacture. You'll probably get out

54

alive, but maybe not. If it all falls apart, we'll deny knowing you."

"There's the stick. Where's the carrot?

"There isn't one."

I swallowed. "If there were money involved ..." I began.

Dick interrupted. "Then you'd just be another whore like me."

"You don't seem to mind making money off your patriotism."

"You have no idea of the depth of my self-loathing. Not only am I universally despised, but I judge myself even more harshly than do my enemies, who are legion. Facebook disgorges a steady torrent of calls for me to stand trial at The Hague. Bush is pitied, but I am reviled. Americans don't mind being lied to if the person lying is cute or somehow attractive to them. Reagan got away with Iran-Contra by just smirking and denying everything. My lip, however, is curled into a permanent sneer. I may be many things, but I am not cute."

"Why don't you just retire and let somebody else fight the good fight?"

"Nobody has the guts to stick with it. We have worked hard to keep the populace in a permanent state of anxiety. It takes perseverance and imagination to keep changing the details of precisely who is our enemy this month, or week. The public has a short attention span. They're easily bored. Do you know how long it took to sell them on Saddam Hussein? Half of them are still confused about the difference between Osama bin Laden and Obama. Heck, they'd rather watch reruns of *Full House* than try to figure out who we're bombing this week and why. No, it takes a lot of creativity to keep America chomping at the bit."

I had to admire the guy. He showed pluck. Most people would find themselves to some degree cowed by the sheer volume of venom they faced with each new day, but not Dick C.

Those who lack his self-confidence do not warrant his attention. I found him both admirable and pathetic, but I secretly feel that way about a lot of people, and co-dependence makes me want to help people like him save face if at all possible. Truth is, I felt sorry for Dick and his over-supply of pluck, and I would stand up for him if he asked me to, merely because I was afraid he would ultimately find himself alone, growling, hissing and swatting while his accusers and detractors closed in.

Fortunately for all involved, higher ups in the administration nixed Cheney's offer to me, and I was given a few hundred dollars compensation for my time. I promptly used this sum to purchase an extremely cheap air ticket to the nearest Third World country, in this case Nicaragua.

MEMO
Re: Our Future

From: The Executive Committee

To: Everyone on our list

We have stopped making progress. They are onto us. Only a change in strategy will allow us to move forward.

This pretending to be reasonable isn't working. Ever since World War II, we have been trying to play the role of the good guy. Nobody cares. Nobody respects a good guy. Only a strong man will do. Will they expect him to be greedy, intolerant, self-serving and despotic? Of course. What real strong man wouldn't be?

Enough with the college professors, the reasonable wimps, soft-spoken and erudite. We don't need Atticus Finch, we need Huey Long. We don't need Eugene Debs, we need Il Duce.

Even though it might not yet appear to be the case, we are suffering from a crisis of leadership.

We need to find a real bully, a real idiot, and elect him President. He can then appoint other bullies and idiots to serve under him. Power and stupidity flow along the same channels.

Of course, we can't say this is our strategy, but if we keep our focus sharp and our intentions murky, we can accomplish this. Ultimately, brutish behavior comes naturally. Piece of cake, walk in the park, shooting fish in a barrel, stealing candy from a baby.

7. Nicaragua

The capital city, Managua, proved to be a real pit, but getting just thirty miles away made all the difference, and I soon found myself lounging in the courtyard of a cheap hotel, catching up on my reading and swatting flies.

But I was no longer in Peru, Indiana, and even though I had brought myself along for the trip, the change of scene was significant. Yes, I was still me, but I was me in an entirely different place. You could buy sweet corn once a year for a month in Indiana, but here there were tropical fruits for sale year around, and the quality was as amazing as the low price. Here, people spoke only Spanish, but already I felt more connected than I did in Indiana.

A bus trip to Matagalpa got me out of the bloated, decaying capital city where the ruins of the 1970's earthquake still lay on the ground. In the hills to the north, Matagalpa was not Switzerland, it was chaotic and junky, but on a scale less overwhelming than Managua. And my chances or being robbed were much lower.

I checked into a minimal hotel, the kind with ceiling fans instead of AC, and lay flat on my back on the single bed to try to figure out what I was doing there. I'd been pondering that question a lot over the last few months, with no easy answers forthcoming. Fortunately, before

I got too far down the familiar path of self-loathing, there was a knock at the door.

I wish I could say it was a beautiful senorita, but instead I have to admit it was a young man of college age, still wearing his backpack. He also sported a nose ring and a very crude tattoo that ran halfway up his neck.

"Sorry to bother you, but do you have a cigarette I could bum?"

"Sorry. Don't smoke. Come in."

He entered my little room and sat stiffly on my lone chair, keeping the backpack on.

"What brings you to Matagalpa?" I asked.

"No reason. Wandering about hoping something comes to me. Hoping to have occasional bouts of fun."

"That's why I'm here, too. As for fun, have you found any?"

"Very little. Mostly boredom and loneliness."

"Welcome to the club," I barked with forced enthusiasm. "Don't take it personally. It comes with the territory. Surely you're writing a travel blog."

"Me and everyone I know."

At this point, my guest began to pick his nose and then studiously examined his encrusted finger. I pretended not to notice.

"Already graduated?" I asked.

"Eight hours short. It's all bullshit, though. I'm not going back. Who needs another guy with a B.A. in English? No, I'm out here to find the real world, to sample reality on its own terms."

"What do your parents think about that?"

"They're so deluded I can't take anything they say seriously. My Dad is an ex-army officer. My Mom is a codependent nurse. I took a course in psychology. She's a classic codependent with underlying narcissism."

"So how do you afford to travel?"

"Last of my student loan."

We sat in silence for about half a minute. "I gotta find me a smoke. I'm seriously addicted. The cravings come every few minutes."

"This is the place to do it. What do cigarettes cost, thirty cents a pack?"

"Marlboros are fifty. But yeah, it's way cheaper than back home. I'm gonna plant some tobacco when I find a place to settle down. Grow my own. Go natural. Mind if I take this off?" He glanced backwards at the back pack.

I nodded and he let it drop to the ground with a thump. I could only imagine the quantity of soiled laundry it contained, along with a dog-eared copy of *Thus Spake Zarathustra* and a rusted harmonica wrapped in a bandana.

"I thought about switching my major again at the last minute," he confessed, "but I didn't want to start over again with the core requirements. It seemed like everything I wanted to do required math. I hate math."

It began to feel hot in the room. I thought about opening a window, but I thought that might imply that I wanted him to prolong his stay, to settle in and get cozy. So, I stayed put.

"I've always wanted to learn a foreign language or two, but it's so darn hard to memorize all those words and grammar rules. They say if you take acid you can learn a language completely in a few hours. I've taken acid several times but I don't think I got to that point. Maybe I didn't take enough."

"Sounds like a rumor. If it were that easy, why wouldn't everybody do it?" I ventured.

"I once saw purple veins underneath the skin in my face when I stared in the mirror for a long time. I kept wanting to come down but the whole trip lasted fourteen hours. That was no fun. I'd do it again though if it meant I could learn a foreign language."

This kid needed more attention than I was willing to give, so I thanked him for visiting me and promised we would stay in touch. I showed him to the door and let him out. I stood there dazed for a moment, wondering if I should change hotels when there came another knock at the door. It was him again.

"I forgot to tell you that Dick, Condy and Hillary all send their love. I don't know who they are. A guy in the lobby gave me a hundred pesos to tell you that."

"What kind of guy? An American?"

"I don't think so. He might have been German. Or Dutch. Maybe even Russian. He has some kind of slight accent."

"Ok. Thanks."

"You can eat for a whole day here on a hundred pesos."

"I'm sure you can. Ok, thanks for the message." I tried closing the door.

"Your picture is in today's Matagalpa paper. Not the big one out of Managua. Under your picture it says, "Famous Glass Eater Visits our City." What exactly does a glass eater do?"

"Eats glass, I imagine."

"Yeah, but why?"

"I've been asking myself that for a while now. I'll let you know if I come up with an answer."

This time I closed the door and locked it.

I didn't sleep well that night. For one thing, a club started playing Ranchera music with the bass turned way up. Salsa I might have been able to handle, but the strict, Germanic oompah-beat set my teeth on edge. Mexican cowboy music is German in origin. It's Polka music. I guess the Mexican influence in Nicaragua is stronger than the South American salsa tradition.

In the middle of the night, I gave up tossing and turning and went down to the street to see what all the commotion was about. There weren't many people about, just a noisy sound system in a dim club. I peered inside and realized my hotel was above the Matagalpa gay club.

Gay men and women, embracing, dancing, leaning against one another in dark corners. How unexpected. Somehow the terms "gay" and "Nicaragua" had never come together in my consciousness before.

Witnessing such an unexpected side of this banana republic made me feel less far from home. Whether I called Peru, Indiana or Matagalpa "home," I was still just a human being living among others, trying not to mess up too badly and enjoy what was in front of me. This awareness allowed me to calm down. No hurry to accomplish anything. If my friends and tormentors wanted to find me, they already knew where I am. No running away from them.

I went upstairs and slept soundly until dawn.

The next morning, I was ready to go somewhere and do something; but even though that was my sincere intention, as I dawdled over breakfast the where to go and what to do part never bubbled to the surface. So, I waited until lunch and went through the same process, with the same results. By the time night fell, I had lost all impetus to do anything, and dinner found me slowly chewing on rice and beans with shredded chicken that might as well have been pork, and staring forlornly into the distance.

But then I met Claude. And Claude introduced me to Veronica. And Veronica ended up changing my life for the better, an outcome for which by this time I had completely given up hope.

I have always believed that I have a highly-developed sense of intuition, and that most of my problems have come from ignoring it. I can almost always tell the good guys from the bad. But I don't always act on those feelings and impulses, and later I wish I had. Women don't have to be pretty for me to notice them. Neither do men need to be handsome or rich. I trust what I see when I look into a person's eyes.

I have the good sense to respect social taboos, and so it has never crossed my mind to have sex with my relatives, or the wives of my friends. I just don't go

63

there. When I met Claude and Veronica, I thought they were a well-established, reasonably happy couple. Later I found that they had met only recently, didn't really enjoy each other's company, and were only traveling as a couple because it was easier that way.

Claude was French, but he spoke perfect English, as well as Spanish, and was always in a hurry. He spoke so quickly it was hard to keep up with the flow of ideas, even though his elocution was impeccable. I just couldn't listen or think as quickly as he could talk. He was having breakfast at our hotel dining room, the same place that became a cantina at night. I later realized that most of the young women who sat on tables in front of our restaurant were prostitutes, but nothing about their dress or attitude conveyed that at first. When I realized what they were doing there, staring into the street and looking as actively bored as a person can, I realized that I would never in a million years be one of their customers. There was no way I could imagine this as sexy.

But Claude loved the nightlife and the life of the city day or night, and he was to show me the intricacies of what I had been overlooking. He was friends with all the ladies of the night. He knew their boyfriends and husbands. He played uncle to their children.

And even though he was sort of ugly and good looking at the same time, with oversized horsey front teeth and a long, Gallic nose, he thought himself handsome, so others did too. In fact, his complete immunity to the thought that he was not charming is what made him so very charming. He was Cary Grant without the looks.

I first noticed that phenomenon when I was in high school, how sometimes a highly unattractive guy could win the hottest girls simply by acting as if were his birthright. "Of course, women love me. Why wouldn't they?"

Women do not find male shyness or timidity alluring. They might wish a timid man well, but they are not inclined to succumb to his charms, because he has none.

Claude oozed charm. In the days I knew him at our hotel in Matagalpa, he was never without the ministrations of an attractive female. I, on the other hand, rarely enjoyed the same. The ladies of the evening looked at me as if I were a man there to check the gas meter. They knew a non-started when they saw one.

I would smile at one and she would look away, as if something in the street were suddenly more interesting. Later, Claude confessed that he had told them I was a police informant. At first, he admitted he thought perhaps I was, for why else would a man of my age and bearing be living in a cheap hotel in a small, Nicaraguan mountain city?

Later, when I told him that I was simply drifting around the world without purpose or direction, and had spent quite a few days watching people stand in line in government offices just to share our common human condition and develop my capacity for empathy, he started telling people I was mentally ill. It occurred to me that he might be right.

By the seventh day of my stay, I was told that my room would be free the following week, for I had unwittingly qualified for the stay-a-week, get one-day-free promotion. I took this as an auspicious event, and I was right, for on that seventh day Veronica arrived.

Veronica shared Claude's complete disregard for convention in dress and speech. I think her native language was Serbian, but I could never get a straight answer out of her regarding where she came from, for she seemed to have already been everywhere and done everything. She talked a lot about Borneo, and once started singing a song that she said she learned in Paraguay, though it sounded Mexican to me. Her hair was jet black streaked with gray, and she wore it in an old-fashioned bun, which made her appear a Mennonite schoolmarm on acid.

The three of us decided to do some exploring together. Paved roads ended soon after the city limits, and in order to go east one had to first travel on a

65

heavily-rutted dirt road, which then dead-ended at a river. All travel beyond that point was by boat, mostly canoes paddled by half-naked Mosquito Indians. Our impulsive and recently-proclaimed goal was to reach Nicaragua's Caribbean coast, a vastly undeveloped area that contained only one city of any size, Bluefields, which had been founded by English pirates many years earlier.

From there we would journey by a larger boat to Corn Island, and then by a smaller craft to Little Corn Island, where we were promised we would find rare snorkeling and diving, a tranquil stay and untarnished tropical beauty. I wasn't much for beach scenes, but I do like a good adventure, and just getting there promised to be at least that.

The canoe trip proved endless. Four days we spent squatting in a narrow dugout tree log, being poled and paddled downstream. We stopped for meals twice a day, and when it got dark, which comes early in the tropics, we stopped for the night. Claude, Veronica and I entertained each other by telling stories. In the process, got to know each other quite well. The Indians were content just to sit around the fire and stare at us talking to each other. Apparently they knew each other so well they had nothing new to say.

Out in the forest, the night is quite loud. Insects saw, monkeys hoot, and non-vocal creatures move through the undergrowth. Unfortunately, no matter how little I drink before retiring, I still have to go to the bathroom a couple of times a night. I learned to urinate as close to the tent as I dared, for any step farther than absolutely necessary posed an unacceptable risk. One night, when I first let go a stream, something directly in front of me growled. It took all my powers of concentration to finish the job before I retreated to the tent.

Bluefields is as ugly a city as you could ever fear to visit, but it looked like Paris to me by the time we go there. The river had widened as it approached the sea, and our going was painfully slow. It was all I could do

66

not to jump out of the canoe and start running down the banks.

Our canoe arrived late, so we missed the boat for Corn Island, and had to spend the night in Bluefields. The only hotel with air conditioning was relatively expensive for Nicaragua, but after four days on the river we were in no mood to quibble. In the lobby, we met a handsome older American, who looked like the actor Hal Holbrook playing Mark Twain, if Twain had been seven feet tall. This man was imposing, and spoke in an affected voice that sounded like a 1940s-actor doing Shakespeare. What was he doing in Bluefields? A garrulous old bird, full of himself and determined to let some of that spill over on anyone in earshot cornered us the moment we set our bags in our room.

"I have two doctorates and have written seven novels, all of which have been published, some to critical acclaim. Before that, I was a commando in a top secret wing of the United States Navy. You won't read about it in any books, that's how top secret it was. I was in 'Nam for the so-called Gulf of Tonkin incident. That was after I muffed my audition for a film role with Rita Hayworth. By that time, she was already showing signs of Alzheimer's, but I had no excuse other than an extreme hangover from the night before, when I had tried to drink Errol Flynn under the table. He was supposed to audition for the same role, but couldn't stay sober long enough to cooperate. As you may already be aware, Flynn spent his later years drinking vodka and grapefruit juice on a yacht that circled the world as he grew thinner and thinner while the eighteen-year-old girls who kept him company grew juicier and juicier.

"It must have been 1964 when I was first offered a teaching job at Harvard, which I declined, not wanting to find myself cooped up in Cambridge. The Cambridge I longed for is in England, on the other side of the Pond, as it were, where I have a good many friends, many of whom hold me in high esteem, though from afar. It's all there in my memoir, which most people

67

think is pure confabulation, though I lived every word of it.

"And all this happened, sadly, before the invention of the computer, which I helped with but cannot take full credit for. Steve Jobs was an admirer of mine, as was his little friend Woz, for they had been the first to start a fan club regarding my trilogy, *The Silicon Apple*, the title of which later proved prescient."

He went on like this for some time, until we noticed that late afternoon had turned to evening, for darkness comes swiftly in the tropics. After a surprisingly good dinner of fish and roasted vegetables, we bade good night to our new friend, who was still telling his life story to a couple of boys who could not possibly understand him, but were too polite to run away.

The three of us shared one room, and as had been our habit the past few nights, we sat in a circle for a time talking. That's when Veronica told us about her contact with Jesus.

"He appeared to me one morning after I had finished mowing the lawn. I didn't really see him, I just sensed his presence, and saw him in my mind's eye. He was enormous. The size of an office building. And there were two angels, one on either side of him, who were equally large. The strange thing was the feeling I got off him. He was the nicest huge guy you'd ever want to meet. He knew me and cared about me and was delighted by me. I got the feeling that he judged me far less harshly than I judge myself. And he had a sense of humor! A wicked, delightful sense of humor. I could tell all this, though I can't explain how I knew. The only words I heard were in my own voice, inside my head, and they said, 'You don't have to worry about any of this. I'm in charge of everything.' His presence lingered. Even after I stopped seeing him, I could feel him. It was Jesus, though he didn't tell me that. I just knew it."

Claude and I sat in silence for a long time.

"Did he ever come back?" I asked.

"Not yet. But he will. I'll see him again, one way or another. I wonder if we will all meet him?" Claude added.

"I sure hope so. You'd be crazy not to want to. Being in his presence was ecstasy."

I surprised myself by saying nothing. Usually not having a strong opinion makes me talk even more vehemently about subjects about which I care little or know nothing. I guess I envied her for having this experience of Jesus, and for knowing so assuredly what was up in that department.

All the confiding-in-one-another we'd engaged in bonded the three of us together in a way I had not known for years. Not since my undergraduate days had I sat around talking so earnestly about abstract ideas.

The boat to Corn Island got us there without a hitch, but the smaller boat from Big Corn to Little Corn was a roller-coaster ride. The seas had picked up and the boat was piloted by a maniac who obviously imagined himself in an action movie. The boat bucked like a bronco. Every time we slammed back down into the water, I thought the fiberglass hull would split and toss us into the sea. When we arrived on Little Corn, I suppressed an urge to drop to my knees and kiss the sand.

Later, I would be praying for a way out of there, but fortunately, I didn't know that at the time.

The first night on the island, we stayed at a minimal but tolerable set of shabby bungalows. At least that's what I thought at the time. Now, I realize we were staying in the best building on the island. Each of us had his or her own cabin, but accustomed as we were to the group, we instinctively turned to visiting. My bungalow had the biggest porch, so we gravitated there.

The first night, just after dark, the electricity quit, and it didn't come back on until late the next morning. No one seemed surprised.

Everything on the island had been brought over by boat, so it was sold at twice the cost it might fetch on the mainland. Claude bought a big bottle of cheap vodka, and we passed it around. After a few hours, he admitted that he was gay, and that he had once been a Roman Catholic priest. Veronica admitted she had given away twin daughters when she was very young. I admitted to being a professional glass eater. My admission earned the longest pause in the conversation. After what seemed like an eternity, Claude asked, "Why?"

"I've done a lot of different things to make money, but this is the one that seems to work best anywhere and anytime."

"But it is dangerous, yes?"

"Not very. Glass is just sand. You break it down into sand and then your body eliminates it. No problem."

Claude seemed satisfied with my explanation, but Veronica did not.

"How does it make you feel to do that for money?"

"I've had worse jobs."

"You didn't answer my question."

"Proud. Proud and accomplished. Sexy. What do you want to hear?"

"The truth."

"Angry. Why am I the chump who needs to eat ashtrays?"

"And the answer is ..."

"I wish I knew."

"I think you already do know. It's just something you're unwilling to admit."

"Are you a therapist?"

"No, but I've been to plenty."

"You and every other woman I know."

The conversation died, but nobody wanted to go off to bed. We sat and stared at the darkness that was ocean. When you thought about how tiny this island was, and how enormous was the sea it inhabited, it got kind of freaky, which is why I avoided thinking about it or

70

anything else that emphasized vulnerability as much as possible.

The next day proved eventless and made me wonder how anyone, even the most empty-headed young narcissist, could sit around listening to Bob Marley, (the obvious Patron Saint of all island dwellers), sipping beer and watching other twenty-somethings walk by. Everyone wore flip flops and swimming apparel. Getting high, playing guitar and dozing in hammocks was, I swear, the only activity, other than probable screwing after dark. The smell of marijuana was omnipresent. I found myself wondering how these people avoided work, until I realized I was simply their older brother.

Again, when left to my own devices I began to worry about what might happen to those suspended on what amounted to a large sand bar in the middle of a vast ocean. I tried to put it out of my mind.

The next day, however, avoiding thinking about our vulnerability became impossible. The morning began with impressive water spouts, little tornados of sea water that rose to a height of maybe three hundred feet. The sky in the distance was dark purple, but I couldn't tell if the storm was coming towards us or going away. The winds blew from left to right, at right angles to the storm and the island, but then, after a few minutes of calm, they shifted and went from right to left. They also gradually increased in intensity. The big flag at the top of our hotel was flapping so hard it threatened to shred itself.

"Is this a problem?" I asked no one in particular. Claude and Veronica didn't reply. There seemed to be no one out and about, for the beach was empty. The smaller boats had been taken in and the bigger ones lay at anchor, bobbing up and down in the increasing surf. Now there was lightening, but still no thunder. It got very dark. "Is this a problem?" I asked again a little louder.

"Depends on what your level of acceptance," Claude responded.

"My acceptance level is getting lower all the time," Veronica added.

When the storm finally hit, it was preceded by heavy rain coming in horizontally, rain so heavy that even the buckets metaphor failed to describe it. It was a fire hose. We ran inside.

My ears began to pop. I was looking out the windows on the side of the hotel when they bowed out and exploded, the wind sweeping away the glass shards. The first thing to go was the thatched roofs, all of which blew away in a few minutes. The metal roofs took longer to fly off, but fly they did, joining their thatched cousins in the sea somewhere off the other side of the island. It turns out the island is only a mile wide at its thickest, so that was pretty much an instantaneous event.

For a while, the rain was so thick there was nothing to see out the now glass-less windows, but when the deluge suddenly ended, I was able to see a very tall man with white hair standing on the beach, waving his arms and shouting at the sky. Upon closer inspection, I realized it was the man we had seen in the lobby of our hotel at Bluefields, the one who looked like a tall Hal Holbrook. I opened the window to see if I could hear what he was shouting about.

"You call this a storm?" he cried to the howling winds, "this is nothing compared to the storm I endured in 1971 on Fiji. A little community of like-minded souls, a yoga ashram actually, though we had no guru, no official leader, so they elected me head pooh-bah, though against my …"

At that moment, a great wave came up behind him and sucked him out to sea. It happened so quickly I couldn't believe what I was seeing. But he was definitely gone. The beach was vacant.

Fortunately, our hotel was made of concrete and rebar, so the walls and floors remained. When the blowing

72

stopped after a few hours, the sun came out and we were able to see that a great many structures had not been so fortunate. Many palms trees had been snapped in half or uprooted. The air was fresh, the sky blue, and puffy white clouds sparkled under the sun. Unfortunately, anything in the foreground failed to contribute to the calendar photo. The palm trees were denuded, with only a frizzy frond or two still in place. There's nothing sadder-looking than a decapitated palm tree.

We assembled on the beach in front of what used to be the center of town, really just a wide sidewalk that ran from the pier to the city hall.

"I knew he would save us," Veronica said at last.

"Who?" I wondered.

"Jesus. He has a plan for us. Otherwise that would have been it."

I thought about snorting in derision, but then checked myself. What was to be gained by alienating one half of the two friends I had? Besides, maybe she was right. Maybe Jesus did have a plan for me, and I was just too dense to notice.

I guess it's going to be up to Jesus to call my attention to whatever clues he's leaving. I can't follow the breadcrumbs if I can't see them.

But He knows that. He knows more about me than I do. Every hair on my head is counted, and God knows somebody should be counting them, because they're falling out fast.

"Now where?" I ventured.

"Someplace else. Someplace lucky," Veronica offered.

"We're already lucky. We're still alive. I bet some people who lived here aren't so lucky," Claude said.

Indeed, there were people walking around crying. Maybe they were looking for lost family members or pets. I remember there had been a large flock of chickens at the house next door, but now I saw no sign of them. Not a feather remained.

"I've got an idea! Let's ask Jesus," Veronica fairly shouted. Claude and I smiled weakly at one another.

"Go ahead, ask," I said.

"Jesus, we need some guidance here. We need to go somewhere else, but haven't got any idea where. We're willing to do whatever we think you're asking of us, but you've got to let us know what that is. Anybody else want to say anything?"

Claude and I shook our heads.

"Well, that's it then. Now we wait for an answer."

We waited until the sun got too hot, and then we sat underneath the awning of the city hall, which, being made of concrete, still stood. About twenty minutes later, a boat pulled up alongside the pier and two men in naval uniforms disembarked. They walked quickly towards us.

"Are you Americans?" one asked.

"Yes," we all said at once.

"We've got orders to evacuate you to Tegucigalpa."

"But that's Honduras. Why not Managua?"

"We don't question orders. You have luggage?"

We were holding the few bags we came with.

"Come on then."

We followed them to the boat and within seconds we were whizzing across the waves at the same speed we enjoyed upon our arrival. I kept trying to brace myself for every slam, but soon gave up, and just let my fillings begin their process or rattling out of my mouth.

Unfortunately, this went on for some hours, way too many hours to keep track of. It made the peaceful canoe ride with the Indians seem like paradise. I kept trying to talk to either of the two men who picked us up, but could not made myself heard over the roar of the engines. It seemed that this was some sort of racing

74

speed boat that had been retired from competition and was now being used to rescue stranded Americans.

We arrived just before dark. The officers told us that their mission had now been accomplished and we were now on our own. They suggested a motel, which seemed pricey by our standards, so we found another favored by backpackers, a group, which apparently, we had joined without knowing it.

Our motel was ok, though it smelled strongly of some artificial grape or cherry carpet freshener. Easier to sprinkle that stuff around than really clean the carpets. There was a dining room/bar, and it was open when we arrived. A Honduran teen girl staring at her cellphone at one end of the bar, and at a table in the center of the room sat an old guy nursing a beer and sort of paying attention to the TV, which was playing what I imagined to be a rerun of last night's *Honduras Has Talent!*

We ordered cokes and a beans and rice dish, with shredded chicken. The old guy turned to us. He wore a patch over his left eye, a ragged hat pulled halfway down his forehead, and his teeth were a convincing shade of dark brown.

"You the Americans from Little Corn?"

"Yes," Veronica said. "How did you know?"

"The man you want to see gave me some instructions for you. He said wait here for further instructions."

"Who is this man?" Claude asked.

"You'll know him when you meet him. He's been waiting for you. Knocking patiently at the door, as it were."

"What does he want with us?" I added.

"His exact words were, 'Don't do anything until you hear from me.'"

"That's a Bebop song from the forties."

The old guy went back to watching the TV.

"He's talking about Jesus," Veronica whispered.

75

"You mean we're on a mission from God?" I whispered back.

"Darn tootin'," she hissed. "This is the real deal."

"I wonder if Honduras is dangerous. I thought I heard of it described as the murder capital of the world," Claude mused.

"This place ain't so bad," the old man said, turning away from the TV during a commercial break. "Nicaragua is safer, because they don't allow our DEA free reign. Here, they just roll over and let us do whatever we want in exchange for foreign aid benefiting the right people. Limiting the supply drives up the price of drugs, which makes them more profitable to sell, so the place is awash in drug runners, even though the biggest dealers of all are in the government. Don't buy drugs, you'll probably be ok."

I noticed when he turned back that the eye patch was now on his right eye. I whispered this fact to Veronica, who nodded vigorously.

"You're Jesus, aren't you?" she said.

"And you're Veronica. You studied for a doctorate in physics, but no professor wanted to take you on as a thesis advisor so you left with a master's degree that entitled you to do absolutely nothing. You think you're smarter than most people and you're right. You have nothing but contempt for hippies and artistic types who don't know much about science. You're all for nuclear power and GMO crops, which puts you at odds with most of the people you come into contact with, especially young people who have never studied anything more rigorous than poetry or women's studies. You're angry with most people and all men. How did you know me?"

"I've been getting bliss rushes from your divine presence. We're at your service. Honored to meet you. Want to do a good job for you."

"Thanks. I wish I could say more people felt that way. Most people are pretty angry with me because something they expected would happen didn't. Their plans

76

didn't work out. That's the thing about plans. When you're making plans that involved millions of people, not everybody gets to have it their own way. You each gotta take turns being right. Sometimes it's not your turn yet. Learn to live with that and you got it made."

"So, what is your plan for us?" Claude asked a bit rudely, I thought, given the circumstances.

"Chill, Claude. It will all become apparent in due time. There's an interesting volcano you can climb a few miles from here. It's mostly dormant, but every once in a while, it burps out a cloud of hot gas and pumice. Good day hike."

I was having a hard time staying in the present moment. This all seemed to nutty to believe, and yet at the same time profoundly real. As a child during the fifties, I had been educated by nuns, and taught to fear the Second Coming, mixing it up with the threat of nuclear annihilation by the Soviets. The idea that Jesus would turn out to be Burl Ives took some getting used to. I half expected him to pull out a guitar and start singing *Jimmy Crack Corn.*

"Why are we supposed to love you?" I found myself asking.

"You get to love me. If you're lucky, you know about me and you want to love me. Once you've experienced me even a little, it's torture to be without me. That's the thing most people don't know yet. It's your job to get to know me and then tell others to do the same. If they want to be happy, to live in peace, it's the only way. The good news is there's no alternative that isn't horrible. Faith is the only way up and out."

"Good act my friend. Hilarious. Understated, clever. I have to hand it to you. Even your getup tells a story. But we're not stupid enough to believe what you're telling us," Claude said.

"I am," Veronica piped in.

"Me too," I echoed, not entirely sure why I was so convinced.

77

At that moment, we looked at the each other and knew this was it, true love, and for some reason I was sure we would spend our lives together. It felt like an invisible horse had kicked me in the stomach. I knew this road was going to lead somewhere important, but I wasn't sure I had the nerve to go for the ride.

Jesus chuckled. "It doesn't matter how long it takes you to come around. You'll get there eventually. There's all the time there is. No, 'Hurry, Sale Ends Tomorrow.' This isn't a race. It's the way things really are and always have been."

Claude was getting upset. "If I thought you weren't completely out of your mind, I would call you out on this bullshit you are serving up. But instead I will laugh at you. Ha. I laugh at you and the preposterous things you are saying."

The old guy didn't register a reaction. He looked like he was thinking about something else.

"I'm drawing men gently to myself. That's the only way it's gonna work. You come when you're good and ready and not a moment sooner." Then he went back to his beer and started watching TV again.

Claude, Veronica and I looked at each other and then quietly left. I wanted to say something to Jesus like "Nice meeting you," but it sounded too trite. Either he was the real deal or not, so nothing I could say at this point would make a bit of difference. If reverence and awe were called for, they weren't in my current vocabulary.

The three of us rendezvoused again, this time in Veronica's room.

"I guess we'd ought to look into long-term rates. And stop wasting money on privacy. This might take a while."

"Claude, what will you do?" I asked.

"I do not know. Surely, I will not remain here long. There is a decided lack of touristic beauty."

78

"Infinite beauty requires infinite patience," Veronica said, sitting on her suitcase.

"Something I admit I lack, Especially at this moment. Well my friends, good luck to you and your new associate. Together, may you save many souls."

Claude left the room, leaving Veronica and I alone. Veronica suddenly looked very tired.

"I've never really enjoyed the company of men, but I've spent most of my life in some sort of relationship with them. I thought with Claude it would be different, and it is. Not better, just different," she said.

"Men are so unconsciously self-centered. It never ceases to amaze me that they can't see how their boorish behavior affects others, especially the women in their lives. I guess they just don't care. For some reason, they feel they have a right to their opinions and the emotions that drive them, and that it's a sacred right. Not open to negotiation."

I jumped in. "I could say the same thing about the women I've been with."

"Well then maybe you and I are a special kind of person who attracts emotional bullies."

"I'd have to say there's a good chance that's the case. But maybe we're also bullies in a kind of sneaky way. We manipulate others into being more obviously demanding, but our manipulation is a sneaky kind of demand."

"Believe me, Claude doesn't lose any sleep worrying about how I feel. I guess I'm attracted to his sense of certainty. He's sure he's right. When I was young, I used to be amazed by people who were sure they were right about anything and everything. These people weren't sure because they were smart, quite the opposite. They were sure because they didn't care to investigate complicated questions. As lazy as they are intolerant. These are the same people who are attracted to religion."

"Are you religious?"

"I used to be. Very. Now I'm looking for certainty one way or the other."

"I'm certain that I'm a pretty bad person, if that impresses you," I offered.

"Why should it?"

"Because I'm certain that I'm bad. I'm a liar and a hypocrite, but more than that, and more importantly, I'm lazy. I blame others for everything, never take responsibility for any situation in which I find myself, and I never really accomplish anything. Most people would have been better off if they'd never met me."

"Sounds like self-pity mixed with grandiosity," she said.

Our conversation ran out of steam. We sat there for a few minutes waiting to see if the other person would come up with a new disclosure, but when that didn't happen, we wandered around together for a few hours until we stopped for a meal at a local sidewalk food stand. The man at the next table had a rooster tied to his big toe. The rooster's head was sticking out of a hole in a bag. Far from looking freaked out by his predicament, the rooster looked quite content to be in a bag, as long as his head was free.

That night I ran into Claude again. Veronica and he were usually together, but this time she must have been avoiding him, or maybe me, for he was sitting alone at a café table on such sidewalk as there was, watching traffic. The expression on his face suggested that he was thinking critical thoughts, for it seemed frozen in a permanent sneer.

I ordered a Coke and sat at the table next to his and stared in the same general direction. I tried to smile benignly, a smiling Buddha.

"I have been thinking. Your name is Donald, right? Like Donald Trump? Oh, he is so famous. You Americans are all so proud of your rich, but you're rich and stupid like Donald Trump, am I right? You have no real culture, just imitations of European triumphs that are hundreds of years old."

"Yes, I suppose you're right, in a way. What culture we have is an odd soup of reactions to European culture," I replied.

"I hate America."

"We don't hate France."

"Good, because if you did, you would be even more barbaric than you already are."

"Why are you so full of yourself? And what set you off to be in such a bad mood?"

"We French are born that way. Instead of a smile, a sneer is our birthright. How do you say ... we are *justifiably proud* of ourselves? Our food is the best in the world. Our sense of fashion dominates. We invented democracy. French people are beautiful and sexy, no matter who they are or what they look like. Our language is beautiful. Sexy."

"Is it true that French men only change their underpants once a week?"

"That is a vicious lie spread by Americans! We Frenchmen bathe at least once a week, sometimes more often than that."

"Whether you need to or not."

"Precisely. You Americans are always jumping in the shower and using deodorant creams but to what effect? Can a gorilla shampoo himself into a human? Yet the whole world is awash in your so-called culture. Your television and movies have spread themselves over the planet like a plague."

"Your feelings about this are surprisingly strong."

"We gave you your Statue of Liberty. And what have you done with it?"

"We've tried to be a force for good."

"When you were not being a force for evil. The world will not forgive you so easily for your arrogance and brutality."

"Speaking of arrogance, didn't you people invent the whole notion of 'snotty?'"

"You cannot successfully insult me. I am immune to all things American."

It didn't take Claude long to decide he wanted to return to Matagalpa alone. I didn't blame him. If I hadn't had Veronica and a sense of higher purpose, I wouldn't have remained more than a night in Honduras. The three of us hugged stiffly at the bus terminal, and then Claude was off, riding on yet another colorful Central American vehicle, an old Blue Bird school bus from the States now enjoying a second car career as an international carrier. As it drove away, I saw *Mason City School District* stenciled above the emergency exit at the back.

I don't know how long Claude remained in Matagalpa, but Veronica and I stayed where we were for five weeks before we heard from our new employer. During that time, we busied ourselves with such sightseeing as could be found, learning Spanish, practicing our daily lesson with the hotel staff, and swimming. We became lovers, but at first that didn't seem terribly important. Over time, however, our interest in each other became more profound.

Tegucigalpa does not come to mind when one thinks of water sports, but the nicest hotel in town had a pool, and most times we could use it for free, as everyone assumed, being white, that we were guests. The few times they asked us to pay, we ordered a lavish lunch, and then they forgot payment for the pool use altogether.

Our needs were being met, maybe in mysterious ways, maybe not, but having each other proved a great prize. This being low season, the monthly rent for our humble room came to about twenty dollars American. Veronica and I were so comfortable together we often felt to need to talk at all. I mentally contrasted this to my life with Natasha, with whom I quibbled constantly just to make sure we were both still alive.

82

MEMO
Gotta Quit

From: Hillary Clinton

To: Condoleezza Rice

Even if I become President, I'm going to have to answer for a lot. All the sympathy I earned from not divorcing the bastard over the Lewinsky thing will have evaporated. Ancient history. When the shit finally hits the fan, as it always does, voters are not going to be happy to learn that I've been less than liberal in my political alliances.

Even though we are all aware that there is no substantive difference between our two parties, we must maintain the illusion in order to sustain a popular faith in Democracy. We're the good guys! (Doesn't matter who we are, but that's OK!)

Just saw *The Man Who Shot Liberty Valence* for the second time in fifty years. I remember seeing it at the Varsity when it came out. It's like a cartoon! Lee Marvin is sooo evil, Jimmy Stewart sooo good, John Wayne sooo strong, Andy Devine sooo lazy. A Batman episode has more subtlety. Yet it was compelling. After a decade of Seth Rogan movies, it's a delight to see something that dares to take a dramatic situation seriously. Good to see character actors Strother Martin, Lee Van Cleef and Denver Pyle in their primes. Vera Miles was Sarah's mother. Jimmy was already a little long in the tooth to play himself as a young man but he pulled it off. Most of the movie is a flashback. It's actually more about democracy in action than it is about gunslingers.

What a naïve faith we had in democracy back then. Jimmy, the Duke and John Ford weren't exactly Democrats, as I recall.

83

I love watching old movies. Doesn't matter where I am in the world, I'm back wherever I was when I saw it the first time. YouTube is the best cure for homesickness ever invented. Bill likes old movies too. It's one of the things we shared that kept us together through all the rough times. That and the fact that married people can't be compelled to testify against one another in court.

8. Charity work

We joined a group of doctors from Texas who were here to repair cleft palates, mostly in infants, but sometimes in older children and even a few adults. The children didn't seem as scarred by the deformity as did the adults, who were so permanently ashamed they would not look us in the eye. The cleft-palate problem can range from cosmetic—an attachment of the upper lip to the bottom of the nose, revealing the front teeth— to an opening all the way back from the top of the mouth, making speech impossible, and causing a whistling noise with every breath. We don't see much of it in America anymore because it's routinely corrected in infancy. But here, the scope of the highly disfiguring condition was obvious.

Our jobs were clerical. Sometimes I took the before and after pictures, but most importantly, we kept the records. Many of our clients had journeyed several days by bus or on the back of a truck to get here. We didn't have beds for everyone. Usually at least four family members accompanied every patient, but those relatives and friends cheerfully slept on the ground.

They try to screen the volunteers for these charity operations, but even then, some of the craziest people find their way through to the front lines. One guy I met there was named Derek, a retired optometrist from Iowa. I guess being an optometrist put him in a sort of medical field, which then kind of dovetailed into cleft palates.

85

Back in Iowa, Derek had almost lost his license for asking his female patients to remove their shirts and bras for eye exams. He claimed spinal alignment was a top priority and needed to be checked. Finally, a few women complained and it was brought to the police. Derek spent the night in jail in his home town of Maquoketa. The Iowa Optometry Board declined to censure him or remove his license, saying they thought he had every right to examine his patients the way he saw fit, though he didn't seem to need to check the spines of his male patients. The county declined the prosecute when the Optometry Board didn't weigh in, so he survived kept his license while losing his patients. There was obviously something wrong with the guy. He was a creep. He seemed to derive too much pleasure out of ogling the females that came before his purview, and sought every chance to touch the women and children who came his way.

Nobody else seemed to judge him the way I did, so I minded my own business. He told me about his scandal back in Iowa on the first night I met him, which gave me pause, because I couldn't tell if he was bragging or confessing. I guess everyone here has some sort of un-usual past, or they wouldn't be here at all. Then one morning I noticed he was spending an unusual amount of time with one patient, so I looked over and saw that a young boy with a cleft palate had been brought here by his older sister, a comely lass of fifteen or so.

The older girl seemed to be the one in charge, and Derek was really putting her through the paces, asking lots of questions that seemed to have little to do with the task at hand. My Spanish wasn't as good as his, and I couldn't prove there was anything amiss, but still, I wanted him to know that he was not unobserved. So I just watched him until he noticed me. And after he noticed me watching, I kept watching.

Later in the afternoon, he said something to me, an apparently innocuous comment which I took to mean more. "Cute kids, huh?" he commented as we waited in line at the mess hall.

"It would be shame if their poverty put them at risk."

"That's why we're here, right?"

"I know that's why I'm here. To minimize their risk. Not mine."

Derek sat at a different table, and engaged in an overly animated conversation with the other volunteers.

I'd seen predators before in my travels to Third World countries, and had developed a sense for spotting them. Still, there was nothing I could do that would easily change things for the better, for most of them were too clever to come to the notice of the authorities. Once, a few years back in another Third World country, I remember seeing a pair of German men in their sixties who had taken a couple of early teenage local girls to a swimming pool. The men leered contemptuously as the girls, who had gone as far away from the men as possible in order to talk to each other. At first it seemed to be a grandfatherly relationship, but then when the men grew tired of waiting, they barked to the girls that it was time to leave, and any sense of fun faded. Smiles faded and the girls accompanied their haughty captors to the parking lot.

The cleft palate operation was not a completely safe procedure. Anytime you use anesthetic, there is a danger of death. This crew of doctors had never lost anyone, but there was an incident earlier in the year, in Salvador, where an adult never woke up from the anesthetic. In the less severe cases, they used Lidocaine in combination with another drug, Versed, that simultaneously relaxed and confused you, what they call a *hypnotic*.

Unfortunately, the local teenagers were well aware of our stash of hypnotic and pain-killing drugs, and these had to be safeguarded at all costs. They were expensive and powerful. An overdose by an inexperienced user was highly probable.

One day, it was my turn to guard the safe, and I found myself distracted by a phone call. That's when I caught a teenage boy with his arm in the open door. Our eyes met and I swiveled in my chair and kicked the door shut,

87

pinning his forearm. He howled in pain and then started crying. I imagine he was sixteen at the oldest. At first, he tried to explain that he was simply looking to borrow a pen, but no one believed him. His arm was probably not broken, but the bruising was already beginning to show by the time the police escorted him away.

The general level of poverty and a tradition of lawlessness combined to make Honduras a pretty dangerous place. Hold onto your wallet. Don't go out at night alone. All this took some getting used to, as my travels heretofore had been confined to Southeast Asia, where Buddhism made people gentle. Sure, you could still get your wallet stolen if you worked at it, but in general, there was no comparing the two cultures.

Here we were in relatively violent Honduras, waiting for instructions from Jesus. If you had told me six months ago that this would be my situation, I wouldn't have believed you.

Veronica and I discussed our unusual circumstances at length one night.

"How long are we prepared to wait for these instructions?" I asked.

"I have no Plan B. Do you?" she replied.

"No. But we could come up with one."

"Sure we could. But we've been making stuff up all our lives. Where did that get us?"

"Here with each other. We found each other," I said with surprising sincerity and conviction.

"We were brought together through no plan of our own. Grace. An unearned gift. There are more gifts on the way, if we don't stir up a bunch of shit and then have to deal with that."

"But will we know grace when we see it? I'm not sure. I've had a lot of good things offered to me, I've known good fortune, but usually I've been looking the wrong way when it showed up."

"Everybody worries about not getting it right. That's what faith is for. Stop worrying. He's not playing hide

88

and seek with us. Or if he is, he shakes the bushes so we won't lose interest"

I was to find out the truth of her last statement the next day when she went off to find a shop to repair her sandals. It seems that even in Honduras, the crafts of making and repairing items were in decline. Almost everything was imported from China. Here, where leather abounded, people wore rubber sandals that were so cheap, people discarded their sandals the first problems arose.

Veronica was gone, and I sat at a street side café. A guy at a table across the room looked like he needed somebody to talk to.

He was older than me by a few years, but he had more hair. I guess you could say his lush head of hair was his crowning achievement, because the rest of his body didn't look so hot. His gut was so big he had to sit far back from the table, and though he nursed his beers and drank slowly, I got the sense that he had been sitting there all day, and would still be there at closing time.

"Nothing's really worked out for me. Oh sure, sometimes it seemed like my ship was finally coming in, but then something would happen and I'd be left staring at an empty pier. Sometimes I like to think of my life as a train rather than a ship. I'm a slow-motion train wreck. Plenty of damage even though it's all happening at a shuffle rather than a run."

"Do you ever think drinking might be to blame?"

He guffawed, perhaps a bit too loudly. "Naw, I'm just a social drinker. A lightweight compared to some of these guys. I've never had a hangover! For me, drinking is just something to do, something to pass the time. A few years ago, when I was living in my ex-wife's basement, I let drinking hard liquor take me somewhere I never wanted to go. I'd lost my license for driving while impaired, and I'd have to beg the ex to drive me to Wal-Mart twice a week so I could buy those big plastic jugs of cheap vodka. Two jugs would last me three days. After six months of living there rent free, I

89

decided it was time to honor the real me, the freak who wanted to let his freak flag fly and see the world. Actually, she kicked me out. I passed out in the backyard with my pants around my ankles. Guess I shit myself and was trying to do something about it when I fell asleep in the mud. So here I am, three years later, in this shit hole. But I like shit holes, third-rate places where they'll cut you some slack and it's always Happy Hour. Did I tell you I used to be a chiropractor?"

"No, we've only just met."

"Well I was. Had a good business until I made the mistake of buying an X-ray machine I couldn't afford. Customers didn't want to pay for X-rays, and the lease on that puppy was nearly my normal monthly income. So, I lost the business, lost my customers, and my life became an Edward Hopper painting. To this day, I avoid jubilance. I shun laughter. If I had a girlfriend, she would be Shelly Winters, the fat girl in the movie *A Place in the Sun*. You ever seen that movie?"

"Montgomery Clift?"

"You have seen it. Shelly's the frowzy blonde, first girl who is nice to him in a town where he knows no one. He knocks her up, and then the boss's daughter, Elizabeth Taylor in her prime, unexpectedly takes a fancy to him. So now he's got a problem. How to get rid of the fat girl. That's the story of my life. I'm like Monty. Certain kind of woman has always taken a fancy to me. You know, the ones with low self-esteem. I've had a million of 'em. Can't even remember most of their names. Shirley, Suzy, Annie, they all blur together into one, needy fat girl."

"Been nice talking to you." I started to get up. "I've got to …"

"If this place isn't nowhere, it's right next door to it. Don't you agree? Took me a long time to find a place so cheap and yet overlooked. Places like this can give a guy like us a much-needed break. Not a drop of excitement, but peace of mind by the bucket. Yessir, this is the Shelly Winters of countries, and this little city is the fat girl of towns. Third-rate all the way."

"That it is. Nice talking to you."

I ducked out into the blazing sun and lost sight of him, as he was now sitting in shadow, seemingly frozen in place behind his little table full of beer bottles, thinking about all the fat girls who had once liked him more than he liked himself.

I was standing on the sidewalk, uncertain of which way to go, when Jesus walked by. He wore the same clothes as before, only they were, if possible, even a little dirtier. He sported a headband that looked like it had been made from an old t-shirt.

"I was hoping to find you here," he said. "How's it going?"

"Ok. Still waiting for instruction."

"Good. That's very good. You're not out there rushing from nutty compulsion to compulsion."

"Only in my head."

"That's the way it should be. 'Wait on the Lord and be a good servant.'"

"Where's it say that?"

"Some place. Maybe a Psalm. Read Jonah. He had a hard time following instructions. Thought he knew it all."

"How do you keep everybody coordinated? Most people aren't really determined to do your will, but even those of us who are need to be coordinated. Right?"

"That's the hard part. That's why everybody needs to chill and wait for guidance. Thanks to advertising, most people think it's a good thing to be guided by impulse, by desire. It's not good. It sucks. And impulse-driven life is a complete mess. Instincts on rampage. Everybody's got the same basic instincts, and if they're allowed to run the show, people are in constant conflict."

"I can see that."

"We're like rats all running for the same door."

91

"We?"

"I'm one of you. That's the part most people forget. I'm just like you except I'm also divine. I'm like your older brother who got there before you and wants to show you the way."

"But why does it take so long to find the way? Why is it so hard?"

"That's the plan. Everybody has to come to their own realizations or else nothing really changed. That's the bad news. The good news is that Divine Mercy is more powerful than your ability to mess up. No matter what you do, it will eventually work out, because Mercy triumphs in the long run."

"Why?"

"Because I'm infinitely more powerful than you and a whole lot smarter than you'll ever be. I have your best interests at heart, so you can relax and enjoy the ride, or you can fret and fidget. Up to you."

"It doesn't make any sense that it's so convoluted, so full of trial and error."

"It doesn't make any sense to you. I understand. But there are a lot of factors to consider here, and most of us can't see farther than our own desires and preferences. If you're relatively clever, you put too much stock in your own opinions. Face it, you're not equipped to understand. Later you'll understand more. Until then, relax and let me do my job."

Jesus lit a cigar and lounged back in a chair that looked like it was getting ready to snap out from under him. The sun was in my eyes so I shifted over to be able to be able to look at him without squinting. It was then that I saw the men in the SUV.

Across the street in a parking lot sat an SUV with dark-tinted windows. Three men stood alongside the car looking in our direction. I got the impression there were more men inside the vehicle.

"Look over there," I suggested.

"Satan and his minions. Yeah, they're all over the place. *Narcos traficantes.* Some work for the DEA as well as the cartels. The place is swarming with them."

"Are they after you?"

"Always. They're after you, too, but they still don't know who you are. Yet. Try to keep it that way. Listen, I have another piece of the puzzle for you. Remember Claude?"

"Yeah. What about him?"

"He's an important person for you to stay in touch with."

"He went back to Nicaragua."

"I know. That's where you should be. Only a different part of the country. Ometepe. You belong on Ometepe with Claude and Veronica. It's an island in the middle of a big lake. Twin volcanoes."

"What am I supposed to do when I get there?"

"Await ..."

"... further instructions." I finished the sentence for him.

Patience is a virtue, and I guess I wasn't very virtuous, but I did my best not to complain about my struggles with it. I just thought I would have more time to improve my character. Turns out waiting wasn't optional There always was, and now I know there always will be, no alternative.

"Wait on the Lord and be a good servant," Jesus said. "That's not too hard to understand, is it? Simple concept, hard to put into practice."

"You've got angels ready to zip across the universe at the speed of light to do your bidding."

"Milton said that. Yes, I remember. He was right. 'Those also serve who only stand and wait.' Yes, he got the message loud and clear. Hey look, I gotta split. If you find those guys are following you, then it's time to drop everything and go. I might see you again down here, I might not. But it doesn't matter. Eternity is a very long time. *Hasta la vista.*"

With that, Jesus put on his shades and walked down the dusty street and on over to his motorbike, one those junky Chinese pieces of crap that everybody rides around here and fall apart after one year. As he took off, I saw two SUV's following closely behind. The last view I had of him, he was riding up a hill into the setting sun, his bike spouting oily smoke and whining like a hornet in a bottle.

A few minutes later, Veronica appeared.

"Jesus was just here," I told her. "Said we belonged on Ometepe in Nicaragua, with Claude. Guess we'd better leave tomorrow."

MEMO
New Blood?

To: Those of Us Not Interested in Running for Public Office

From: Those of Us Interested in Controlling the Outcome

Let's face it, we're getting long in the tooth. Our little club is shrinking even as we shrivel. We have to find new talent to throw into this talent pool.

What about finding a TV personality instead of yet another lawyer? Someone who already has the public's ear and eye. The less this person knows about government, the better. An outsider. Someone like a professional wrestler, but not quite that low-class.

America hates intellectuals. The common man assumes they're all communists or fags, anyway. Thanks to Reagan, America also hates politicians. So it can't be someone with a record that can be attacked or resurrected like a month-old sandwich and then shown to the Press.

It could be an athlete, but athlete's get old and lose their panache. It could be woman, but not a woman who is assertive, scorned as a ball-breaker and a hag. Can't be someone who is obviously human. We don't want our leaders to be flawed human beings. We want to be ruled by supermen.

So, look at this as an invitation to throw someone else's hat into the ring. Everyone has some dirt they'd rather hide and we have ways of persuading even the most reluctant public servant to step up to the plate. Who knows, this person might well hit a homer on his first try.

95

9. Back on Ometepe

Claude was sort of glad to see us—even though he pretended not to be—but he seemed genuinely hesitant to believe our claim of divine guidance. We assured him Ometepe was exactly where we needed to be. It only took a day and a half to get there, culminating with a ferry trip across a choppy Lake Nicaragua, with the dramatic cone of *Volcán Concepción* growing steadily larger as we approached.

We found an inexpensive rental at a place called El Porvenir: *The Future*. It bordered the flanks of the dormant volcano, the two volcanoes making up most of the island's land mass. There was absolutely nothing shaking at El Porvenir, but that was OK, because we had nothing to do but wait around. With nothing close by, there was no temptation to go anywhere. We ate, slept and ate again.

Every once in a while, we walked down to the water to swim a little, but there was no attractive beach to hang out on, and the sun was awfully hot, while the lake was warm, brown and lacking in any sort of wave action. So, we rarely bothered to hit the beach. Fortunately, there were plenty of hammocks around, and a stony trail leading up to the other volcano for those restless enough to want to hike. I've never seen much percentage in trudging uphill, especially in tropical heat, but Claude made it to the top without complaint. He said there was a crater full of brown, warm water up there, a little cooler than the lake water, but not terribly more attractive.

Our tranquil days were brief. The guys in the SUV's came at night. I heard them driving up the steep concrete driveway and talking to the guard. Even though I couldn't understand what they were saying, I knew it was time to go. The three of us crept out of our hut and slipped through an open gate in the fence and as quietly as possible. We faded into the woods. With no flashlight and no idea where we were headed, we kept going because we had to alternative. We didn't want to stay where we were and meet our future captors.

After a while, we decided it would be better to stop walking, so we hid in the bushes for hours. Eventually dawn came, and when we returned to El Porvenir the men in the SUV's were gone. Still, we didn't want to risk going back to our rooms so we began to walk the trail that led to the dormant volcano. Roosters crowed. People were out working already, hacking away with their machetes and the infinite amount of green stuff that was growing all around.

We waved and said, "Hola," and most people waved back. After slowly climbing for about an hour, we found ourselves at the lake that Claude had already visited. It was still early morning and pleasantly cool. The other volcano stood in the distance, beautifully lit from the east by the sun, and just as we were admiring the view, it's Platonic Idea of a volcanic cone disgorged an immense chimney of jet-black ash. About twenty seconds later we heard a resounding boom. The sharp report of it echoed and re-echoed from this volcano to the other and back again.

"Thank God we're on the dormant one," Veronica said.

We watched the black smoke blown in two different directions, depending on altitude Within three minutes, there was nothing left to show. Then we heard bubbling coming from the lake. The bubbling stopped. Not long

98

afterward, scores of fish floated up to the surface on their sides. Soon there were hundreds, maybe thousands. The lake must have been quite deep, because it was hard to imagine that many fish living in such a small body of water.

"At least we won't go hungry," Claude said, as he began to use a long stick to retrieve a number of them.

We didn't go hungry, even though we stayed there by the lake for the entire day. Turns out Claude had everything a survivalist would need in his backpack. We had a fire, impaled the fish on long metal spikes, and completed the meal with trail mix and filtered lake water. The entire day we didn't see another person. Usually a constant stream of hikers visited the volcano summit, but today it seemed they were either staying put or had already left the island.

We had no way of knowing that a general alarm had been issued, and that ferry service to the island had been halted, and all boats had been deployed to ferry people to the mainland. Most of the permanent residents chose to stay, but many tourists had already left; and of course, we had no idea if the mysterious men who had come to El Porvenir were among them. Maybe we had overreacted. Who knew?

We weren't sure what to do, so, in accordance with our latest philosophy, we did nothing. The day got warm, then the sun set and it became surprisingly chilly. Howler monkeys howled, or rather, hooted in the trees nearby. Their calls sounded amplified, as if each monkey possessed an internal amplified speaker.

The next day, the dead fish were beginning to smell bad, so we left the volcano, climbing back down a steep trail that ran by a large waterfall. Occasionally, a gap in the trees afforded us a view of the lake below. Still no ferry operating.

When you're on an island, you're acutely aware that you're no longer on the mainland, and that unless you own a speedboat you can't just zip away at a moment's notice. With this mindset, we leisurely made our way down to the water's edge, where the dirt and rock road that circled the island would take us back to the nearest town, Alta Gracia.

Before we made it five minutes farther, a speedboat piloted by a man who looked like he was playing the role of an Italian playboy in a sixties movie pulled up near the shore. Two women with bleached blond hair sat behind him.

"Want a lift?" he called in English.

"Where to?" Claude asked.

"Anywhere but here, I would imagine," the playboy answered.

After wading into water up to our knees, we climbed aboard. The blondes, also wearing Ray Bans, giggled in unison.

Turns out we were headed back to the mainland, but not to the town with the ferry terminal, another one I'd never heard of before, a simple place with fewer than a hundred homes. The Italian playboy pulled alongside and we climbed up on the dock. Then he waved a merry goodbye, gunning the throttle and raced off. The girls smiled and giggled, leaning backwards with the acceleration and waved goodbye.

It was there we learned that political unrest had preceded the volcanic burp by a few hours, and that a state of martial law had been imposed throughout the country. Nobody knew anything for sure, but apparently there had been a coup, and the President was either in exile, prison, or dead.

We had no idea what this news meant for us, and for the moment we didn't care. Even though there was no proper hotel in the town, we were able to secure rooms in a guesthouse, a ramshackle affair with crowing roosters in the yard and laundry on the line.

Claude—not sharing Veronica and my new-found faith in you-know-who—brimmed with plans. He suggested we follow the Rio San Juan east back to the Caribbean, link up with rich people who sailed yachts around the world for pleasure, and sign on as deck hands. He had done the very thing twenty years earlier, and had managed to circumnavigate the globe in a haphazard and informal manner.

We told him we couldn't join him, as we were awaiting guidance from above. Claude didn't say anything for a while, then he ordered a beer and told us what he thought of our new belief system.

"You are delusional because you're stabbing around randomly trying to make sense of your lives. And since you're both in the same place, enduring a crisis, you're supporting each other in your irrational beliefs. But the crisis will eventually pass. Maybe then you will be able to let go of the irrational beliefs. Maybe not. I hope for your sake you will."

We couldn't think of anything to say that would change his mind, or cause him to suddenly want to be a believer, so we thanked him for his opinion and said we were glad we were all together again.

I remembered what Jesus said in the bar in Tegucigalpa. "I draw men gently to myself."

There was an old guy trying to flirt with two women who seemed irritated by his presence. When he looked my way, I nodded and smiled. He appeared European or American, but his nose was crooked in a way that suggested it had been broken long ago in a fight and never property set. After the girls left, he approached us.

"I noticed you arrived on Don Vicente's speed boat. Did he try to hold you up out there? That's his thing. He gives people a ride and then he robs them out in the middle of the lake."

"No, he just gave us a lift."

"You're lucky. Maybe he figured you were so broke it wouldn't be worth his while. I met one couple whom he pitched overboard. They swam the last mile to shore."

"I wonder if there were others who couldn't swim," ventured Veronica.

"That was my thought, too," the old guy added. "Say, would you happen to have enough to buy me a beer? I'm plum broke."

Claude came up with the money. The old guy handed him something and shuffled away.

Veronica sighed. "I think we're going to be stuck here for a while."

"How much did you give him?" I asked.

"I think about forty-five cents," Claude responded. "He gave me this." Claude unwrapped a wad of brown paper. It contained two almost identical rings, rust colored, with an orange stone. One was bigger than the other. They looked like wedding rings of some sort.

"He said these were for you two."

"He said that?" I asked.

"He mumbled it."

Veronica examined the rings. She slipped the big one on my finger and the smaller one on hers.

"Darling!" she cried, ironically.

We hugged clumsily.

Claude looked away.

It had gotten dark in the last few minutes. We were barely able to see one another inside the restaurant. People here get by with little artificial lighting. Electricity is unreliable. Bulbs are few and weak. And when the sun sets in the tropics, it does so in a hurry. No lingering twilight. With the general lack of illumination and clouds, the stars are quite brilliant. I will always remember that view of the constellations and a crescent moon floating above the volcano, still dimly glowing from the last of the setting sun. I felt like something important was happening, but I wasn't sure what it would turn out to be.

The next day, we went down to the waterfront to see about getting a boat back to the island. There were none. Easy, however, to catch a bus going anywhere else in the country. So we caught one headed to Rivas, a short hop away, a city with absolutely nothing to recommend it, but at least it was a city. There was even a hotel with air conditioning, though rooms were as expensive as back in the States. We had lunch there and waited to see how things would turn out. I guess we were once again waiting for guidance, while playing the role of tourists.

Even though it was blisteringly hot day, the hotel patio wasn't too bad, with lots of shade and fans shared by every other table. As happens in a lot of Central and South America, beggars bothered the patrons unless chased away by a waiter. Our waiter was busy taking an order from another table when a toothless, shoeless black man approached. To our surprise, he spoke perfect though poorly enunciated English.

"If you had any idea how much I love you, you'd stop your whining and enjoy every moment of your life," he said, holding out his hand for money.

Veronica gave him a few coins.

"Each and every one of you is the source of immense delight. In heaven, we can't get enough of you. Even when you mess up, it's cute, not creepy."

"Do you have any guidance for us? We're waiting for instruction," I asked.

"Dig the present moment to the max. This is it. This is as good as it gets. There's nothing you need to do that hasn't already been done. This is the fun part. Drudgery is over. You can drag your ass around and mope if you want to, but it doesn't entertain me and it certainly doesn't do much for you."

"We're not deliberately manufacturing misery, "I protested.

"Good, because there's enough of it already. And it's all fake. Stick to the real stuff ..."

Just then our waiter arrived and shooed the beggar away.

"Keep trying to get back to the island," he said as he stumbled back out into the street.

This was not what we wanted to hear. We were so done with the island. As a matter of fact, the charms of Nicaragua were starting to fade. What at first had seemed fresh and revolutionary, now felt shabby and hopeless. Discouraged, we decided to eat and maybe come up with a plan of action. That's when a group of Americans entered and took a table across from us.

"Tell us what you do for a living," the leader asked.

"Is it true you eat ashtrays?" asked his comrade.

"Can you eat one now?" a third inquired with a sneer.

"Sure. I do it if others bet I can't. How much are you willing to wager?"

They snickered and looked at each other. Soon the boldest in the bunch wagered one hundred dollars that I couldn't eat the ashtray sitting on the table in front of me. I made a big deal out of staring at the astray in mock fright. It wasn't especially large, but I stared at it solemnly, even managing a comic gulp.

His friends soon followed suit. I asked them to give the money to the bartender for safekeeping, and then I asked for a paper bag and a hammer and began the process of reducing the ashtray to powder. Veronica stared at me, as this was the first time she had seen me in action. I didn't especially care for the expression on her face, but then I didn't especially care to be going back to work, except for the fact that we needed the money. Three hundred dollars would last us almost a month here.

I wondered if these Americans were the men who had come to El Porvenir the night of the fish kill. They certainly weren't tourists, as they had an air of SWAT team about them that just wouldn't dissipate no many how beers they drank. The streets here were filled with a mix of people, but the wealthy certainly stood out compared to the rest of us. And these men looked as if they hadn't missed a meal in a long, long time.

104

Pulverizing the ash tray took a long time, and usually my audience waned after fifteen minutes, though there was so little going on here that I held their attention for a good half hour. Veronica stared at me the entire time, and in that stare I read a variety of emotions. Blame, shame, sorrow, and finally compassion. No, it wasn't easy being me, but I could have told her that if she's just asked.

As I imbibed yet another glass ashtray, I had time to think. Nobody was asking me to do any more than to pulverize and consume. Freed from drudgery and novelty, the mind can become delightfully creative. I began to wonder what might be the eventual import of these recent developments.

America was in flux, a bigger flux than anyone with something to lose would care to admit. Desperate characters stood waiting in the wings, ready to take center stage. Even so-called *liberals* were actually more conservative than anyone I would care to be associated with. Hillary and her friends liked to play the role of liberal, but she seemed quite at home with the people whose response to the World Trade Center bombing had been to invade Afghanistan and then Iraq.

I had always been suspicious of those who claim there is a Dark Government, and that the characters we see, the ones we actually get to vote for, are merely puppets, but here in a far-away Banana Republic, surrounded by Squares with crew cuts and walkie-talkies, I felt like I should have trusted my instincts all along. These people are the enemies of freedom. Always have been. Ironic that Reagan dubbed the thugs he hired to prolong the Nicaraguan revolution Freedom Fighters. He said they were the "moral equivalent of our Founding Fathers."

If you're looking for evidence to confirm your biases, you will find it eventually. Even a stopped clock displays the correct time twice a day. Looking back and reviewing the last few years, I could see how I had chosen to ignore facts and occurrences that could have prompted me to make different choices, to take a different path, but that I discounted the facts because to heed them would have taken too much work. It would have demanded making difficult decisions. So I coasted along, claiming I was keeping an open mind when actually I was just being lazy. Now I felt anxiety and fear, casting about wondering who to blame.

No one was to blame but myself, I concluded. The warning signs were always there, I had simply chosen to ignore them. Even forty years ago, everyone knew Nixon was not only a crook, but evil. What kind of man needs to proclaim, "I am not a crook?" Only liars assure their victims that they are not lying. Only swindlers proclaim, "Trust me, this is a good deal for you."

Nixon was a crook, Kissinger a whore, Reagan an idiot, Bush One a Creep, Clinton a Whore, Bush Two an Idiot; and there was no reason to assume that a better person was on his or her way to the White House.

In fact, we may be in for much worse. This may get much worse before it even starts to get better.

No one wants to face unpleasant facts if there's a way around doing so. Far more pleasant to believe bullshit if it buys you a reprieve from anxiety or the pressure to take action.

As I was thinking, and grinding glass into powder, I noticed a boy sitting across the room staring at me as if I were the most interesting person he'd ever seen. Veronica was on the other side of the room, so I had my fan club in stereo. The men who I was counting on to pay me came and went, absorbed in their own activities, but my fans were content just to watch me go about my tedious job.

This boy was an angel. Big black eyes and curly hair. He looked like one of those cherubs you see around the fringes of an Italian church painting. Sometimes he looked directly at me and sometimes he pretended to look away but was still watching from an oblique angle. I wanted to talk to him but didn't want to drag him into this, not knowing for sure what lay in store for me. For some odd reason, a poem I had memorized in high school popped into my head as I saw him there in the corner. It was a Wordsworth poem.

> *My heart leaps up when I behold a rainbow in the sky:*
> *So was it when my life began,*
> *So is it now I am a man,*
> *So be it when I shall grow old or let me die!*

As I watched him watch me, I remembered that America, the bully who made the world safe for democracy at the expense of poor people all over the globe, who clandestinely bombed Laos every day for ten years, killing ten percent of the population, who let Nixon deliberately interfere with Vietnam War peace talks that could have ended the war before the 1968 election, so that he might be elected and take the credit, thus prolonging the war five more years.

Kissinger, who went on a visit to South America, assuring the generals of Argentina and Chile that we would not interfere with however they chose to take care of their *Communist Problem,* thus dooming those countries to an orgy of murder and torture that ravaged their fragile democracies in ways that took decades to heal.

I thought about all the foreign military thugs we'd educated in torture and mass murder at the School of the Americas in Georgia, all the aid we gave the Philippines and Indonesia to kill whomever their leaders deemed Communist, the mass graves in El Salvador, the Guatemalan civil war that lasted twenty years after we destabilized their democratically elected government ... and eventually I found that I had stopped pulverizing the ash tray, that my hands were now balled into fists, and that I was weeping.

I didn't know who I hated more, the people who had been in charge or people like me for letting it happen.

I knew what was coming down all along. Even when I was in elementary school I could spot a bully across the school yard. Ehrlichman, Haldeman, G. Gordon Liddy, Oliver North, John Ashcroft ... creeps, dullards, frat boys, golf-playing white guys who hated all dark-skinned people and fags. And even now they were still in charge of almost everything.

Besides their smug sense of entitlement, what did I despise about these men? Their duplicity. Although I'm sure they thought their lying was altruistic, necessary because of the flawed world they lived in, they were still liars. And then I thought about the lies I have told, the people I allowed to assume what I knew not to be the case, the people I manipulated by hiding a hidden motive under a more acceptable one. And each memory came at me like a spear.

I sat at that table in that little cafe, watched over by an angel disguised as a Nicaraguan boy. I squirmed in my chair, reviewing a life in which I had, "pierced myself with many sorrows," as the Apostle Paul described in his letter to Timothy. I thought of the women who had expected to be loved by me and were not; the students at my University who had expected to receive a valuable education and instead got a lesson from the school of hard knocks. It was agony.

Sometimes I think it would be easier if eating this ground glass could scour my insides and let me start over.

Then I began eating the sand. Usually, I washed each mouthful down with a drink, and since I hadn't been drinking alcohol for a while, I chose Coca-Cola diluted with water. Eventually I would switch to just water, but the eating took longer than the pounding, and I would be a this for several hours.

Veronica watched me, shooting a wan smile my way every once in a while. The three men had begun to argue among themselves about something unrelated to me, so I didn't notice when two of them left. Finally, the leader of the group gave me his undivided attention and spoke. "You seem far too clever for this sort of thing. There must be something going on inside you that makes you think this is all you deserve. I guess it beats some self-destructive behaviors, but it doesn't add up, at least to this observer."

I didn't reply, but kept eating small amounts of sand.

"You could help your country if you like. That group of men you despise? They like you for some reason I can't surmise. Dick, Don, even W are hoping you'll stand up for our country when the time arrives. Well, I'm here to tell you that time is now. Hillary and Condy both want me to remind you that we all have to do our part. Do you agree?"

I didn't know what he was driving at, so I just nodded and kept swallowing.

"Let me introduce myself. I'm Al Crowley, Special Forces. We're excited by all the possibilities here and were hoping you could carry the ball into the end zone for us. They've found a way to turn nuclear waste into glass. Deadly plutonium can be rendered almost inert by being turned into a kind of glass. We want you to show the public that nuclear energy can be safe. We want you to eat that glass. We want you to ingest the entire annual output of radioactive waste from an operating plant and we want you to do it on nationwide television. It's been vitrified, turned into glass, and made inert. Can't hurt you."

I said nothing but Veronica got upset. "Who the hell do you think you are?" she said, more loudly than I'd heard her say anything in the time I'd known her.

"Just a fellow patriot," he replied. "Just another guy doing his job. Call me Al."

The more I saw of this guy, the more I liked him. I still didn't care much for the people who sent him, but that didn't mean they had all been painted with the same brush. But I did have to admit that if this were a painting, it was one by Hieronymus Bosch.

The more I saw of this guy, the more I liked him. I still didn't care much for the people who sent him, but that didn't mean they all had to be painted with the same brush.

It took five more hours to finish the job. Just before dawn, the bidders examined the table at which I'd been sitting, and realized the ashtray was gone. The other two guys never came back, but the one guy handed me the cash, and then said "I hope you'll give what I said serious consideration. They're waiting to hear from you."

Veronica and I staggered back to our rented room, drunk with fatigue. When we fell into bed with our clothes on, we both stared in silence at the ceiling. Something was crawling up there, probably a gecko. I thought about turning on the ceiling fan to scare it away, but then I closed my eyes and forgot all about the gecko until I woke hours later to someone pounding at the door.

MEMO
Divine Mercy

From: Jesus

To: Kissinger, Nixon, et al.

This is your Lord and your God speaking. I've been watching this drama unfold, and it's finally coming together the way you had hoped it would. I'm glad for you, for it's what I want as well. Your will is my will. I want you to be happy, all of you, not just the rich and crafty. I want all of creation to enjoy life. If that means getting what they want, then I want them to have it.

Too bad you believed the lie that our wills are opposed, that I don't want what you want, that you could have more fun if you opposed me. Exactly the opposite is true. I'm on your side. Always have been.

Nixon is cuteness personified, but he's the last one to believe it, even if his Lord and God knows it to be true. Deep down Cheney is as sweet as people get. Hoover is a Teddy Bear. But try to get them to see it!

10. The Climax

It was them again. The Frat Boys, the CIA. The guy who had done most of the talking was at my door with the other two guys acting as lookouts a few yards away.

"They want an answer. There's a chopper with the glass from the reactor waiting for you at Gitmo. They'll bring it down here the moment you say yes."

"What's in it for me?"

"Besides helping your country?"

"You mean helping the nuclear power industry."

"Solar and wind ain't gonna do shit. Our energy demands are already a hundred thousand times bigger than that. We're stuck. The air heads and hippies don't want to hear about it, but it's true. You can help us prove that we've got the hazardous waste thing covered."

"Well, what's in it for me?"

"More money than you've ever seen before or will again. And you'll be famous. You can charge more for eating ashtrays, or give it up and go into a new line of work. Or retire here and never work again. Up to you."

"I want to live here. On the side of that volcano. I want to own a few acres of land, have a simple bamboo house with a thatched roof. I don't need a lot of money to do that."

"OK, give the extra money away. Up to you."

113

Veronica indicated she wanted to talk to me in private. I told him we'd get back to him in a few minutes and closed the door.

"He's right, you know," she said once we were alone. "Nobody wants to face facts, but we can't just listen to a bunch of brainless hipsters and airhead dreamers. We've got to find a way to deal with nuclear waste and stop burning hydrocarbons."

"Where did these strong opinions come from? How come I never saw this side of you before?"

"We don't know each other that well. Just because we like each other doesn't mean we're the same person. If these guys are going to give you a bunch of money to eat glass, take the money. Eat the glass."

"What if it kills me? It's radioactive."

"It won't kill you right away. It'll kill you in thirty years. By then something else will have killed you already."

"I thought you were on my side."

"I am. I'm on our side. This is probably why Jesus asked us to come here."

"Jesus. Forgot all about him. Yeah, maybe you're right."

"We don't need to know what's going on," she continued. "We just need to have faith that He does, and that he's got our best interests at heart."

"He's got a plan."

"Maybe yes, maybe no. He could also merely be winging it. But if so, he's better at it than we are."

When I told the guy I'd do it, things started to happen really quickly. A very nice speedboat whisked us back to the island and we soon found ourselves back at El Porvenir, the idyllic guest house on the flanks of the volcano, which we had last seen in the middle of the night when we slipped into the woods to avoid capture.

Within hours TV crews began to arrive. BBC, Al Jazeera, CNN, NHK, Deutsche Welle. Fox News sent a legion of blonde bimbos. Then the black helicopter arrived at a helipad I hadn't noticed before. The beautiful vegetation surrounding it was momentarily flattened by the prop wash from the spinning blades.

Cameras rolled as soldiers carried the silver sarcophagus towards me. Reporters who tried to ask me questions were stopped by my handlers and given a list of talking points, which I had no part preparing. I didn't mind. This wasn't my deal, it was theirs. I was simply the guy who was going to eat twenty pounds of nuclear waste fused into a blob of dark purple glass.

Set up took a long time. They gave me a large mallet to begin the operation and two smaller hammers to whack the chunks with. As I hovered around the honey wagon, which in this case was a grill set up to cook Nicaraguan street food, I was wary of spoiling my appetite. A reporter from Al-Jazeera approached. Quite a beauty with the biggest mane of jet-black hair I'd ever seen, she started whispering questions to me.

"Is this the biggest object you've ever eaten? Is there a sexual thrill attached to eating glass? Why aren't you afraid of being poisoned? Who was your favorite Beatle?"

"My favorite was John. He was the driving force and personality behind the group. The others were just along for the ride. Though Paul was a good compliment to John, his talents were small by comparison."

She nodded and waited for me to reply to the other questions. I tried to think of something succinct or clever to say, but couldn't. Fortunately, I was rescued by a man with a walkie-talkie and a commanding presence.

"They need you on set," he said both to me and his walkie-talkie.

When I sat down behind the purple blob, all eyes were on me. Even though the sun was bright, they had found it necessary to use bright reflectors which focused the rays right into my eyes. I could barely keep my eyes open, but my request for sunglasses had been denied for fear it would make me look sinister. The image I was to convey needed *warmth*.." Indeed, it was quite warm there in front of the cameras.

Fortunately, they didn't want me to talk, so I had no microphone. All around me, a steady cacophony of voices and languages commented on my activity as I began to break down the purple blob, first using a sledge hammer and then a smaller hammer on the pieces. Even I could hear their forced enthusiasm wane as the process dragged on. Sexy this wasn't.

Six hours into it, I began to eat. At first, I couldn't notice any difference between the purple glass and an ordinary ashtray. Certainly, it didn't taste different, but it was all I could do not to let my imagination get the best of me and detect a warmth coming from my gut. Surely, they wouldn't have gone to all this trouble to deceive me and the general public.

Veronica, who had been sitting on the sidelines watching with increasing concern, came over.

"How is it going?" she asked.

"Same as usual, except I'm trying not to let my imagination run riot."

"He wouldn't have sent us here if this was a bad idea."

"Oh, Him. Yeah, I guess you're right, or else we're both wrong, in which case I'm eating a nuclear reactor just for the heck of it."

The sun was setting and the TV lights seemed all the brighter. By now, the best looking of the reporters had tired of the affair and retired to their dressing rooms, little campers and motor homes. A mariachi band hired to pep things up waited in the wings for permission to play. They seemed puzzled by what was going on. I had to suppress the desire to take them aside and tell them they were not alone in their puzzlement.

The rumbling started just after the moon rose. At first, I thought it had to be some sort of construction noises, but then I remembered that there was nothing being built on this part of the island, and the volcano we were on was the dormant one, so it couldn't be that. But what about the other volcano, the one a few miles away?

The rumbling noises came and went for the better part of an hour, until a sharp explosion got everyone's attention. Suddenly, all cameras swiveled toward the overlook, with some camera operators removing their cameras from their tripods and carrying them on their shoulders. From where I was sitting, I couldn't see the volcano directly, but I could see a red glow of the eruptions flickering on the people standing along the road in front of me.

I was beginning to feel something. A light-headedness, an elation that made people seem impossibly funny and, dare I say it, cute. Suddenly everyone seemed equally endearing. I felt compassion for them all, an avuncular feeling, a diffuse and non-specific love. I wished them well. I was delighted by their efforts and activities, all childishly playful in the face of what we were actually experiencing. How can you compare a volcanic eruption to a man eating ground glass as a publicity stunt? One has actual gravitas, the other is patently silly.

My new mood allowed me to eat much more quickly. I now swallowed the slurry with gusto. No one was paying attention to me anymore, as the eruption had upstaged me. Someone even switched off most of the lights so it became much more pleasant. I was enjoying this more than any other work experience in my glass eating career.

The ash began to fall, making its presence known through the leaves of surrounding vegetation. Falling pumice reminded me of ice rain back in Iowa. Not hail, but frozen rain, black ice, the kind that renders streets and sidewalks so slippery that all travel becomes impossible. Suddenly, the technicians scrambled to protect the cameras. Anchor people retired to their dressing rooms, all except for one blonde bimbo from Fox, who, drunk on excitement, zipped around babbling at anyone who might listen.

"This is an actual event! This is real news!" she kept gushing, getting more excited with each repetition. Veronica suddenly awoke and pointed at the lady, laughing. She waved at me to make sure I saw her too. I waved back, finding both Veronica and the Bimbo to be impossibly cute.

At that moment, I saw another reporter, the one I assumed was German and working for *Deutsche Welle*, interviewing a tall man with white hair. It was him again! The Hal Holbrook look-alike. They were maybe thirty feet away from me, but I could decipher his precise, pompous diction at this distance.

"This eruption is nothing compared to the ones routinely given by the Italian volcanoes. Etna and Vesuvius are constantly erupting, disgorging both molten lava and incredible amounts of ash. Pumice is the precise term. I'll never forget when I was in Mexico scouting locations for John Huston's first attempt at *Under the Volcano*. There we were in Michoacán, standing in the middle of a cornfield, when the very ground about our feet began to bubble and heave. I had been offered the lead role in the picture, the one later taken by Albert Finney when the film was finally made, years later."

I wanted to hear more, but could not make out the sounds as a helicopter nearby had started its engines.

How had he survived being sucked out to sea on Little Corn? I wanted to ask, but we were in a hurry to leave, and those about me were moving with such a sense of urgency that made me think this was no time to dawdle. There was still sand to be consumed.

My handlers approached and told me to pack up. By now I had eaten most of the ground glass. They advised me that we were going to evacuate to the mainland.

"What do we do with the remaining sand?" I asked.

"We'll get a doggy bag," the leader replied, solemnly.

I felt nothing but compassion for him and was deeply touched by his care.

Veronica, the doggy bag, and I scrambled to the helipad just as a few hundred howler monkeys leaped from the branches of a nearby tree, hooting as they landed and scurried along the ground. They were followed by a dozen young people in yoga pants fleeing a New Age resort nearby. We climbed aboard the chopper, whose engines were now revving faster and whose blades were already turning.

As soon as we took off, I could see the scope of the eruption. Huge clouds of jet-black smoke and ash were pouring from the mouth of the volcano, while red fires from below sporadically shot above the rim. We were lucky to get away, and my gratitude caused tears to well in my eyes. Gosh, this was great! Could anything be better?

My excitement was mixed with a rare a novel sense of peace. I was calmly excited, if such a thing were possible. Choked with gratitude, speechless with wonder, I beheld the maelstrom of fire and smoke below.

That's when I realized it was time to jump. Our curious pilot was taking us on a route right over the crater. If ever there was a time to experience jumping directly into an erupting volcano, this was it. How fortunate that it was all coming together like this! My hand gripped the bag of sand even more tightly. I asked if we could slide the door open for a better view. Despite the noise of the motor and the fact that they were wearing headphones, the men in charge consented. I slid the door open. Veronica leaned over for a better view. We both stared down into the cherry-red circle, with swirling black smoke pouring upwards. I began to feel such elation as I had never tough possible. What better end could one imagine for such a wonderful life?

Before I could jump, I lost consciousness, and in the process relaxed my hold on the bag, which fell directly downward and into the fire. The crew caught me before

119

I fell, and the pilot banked sharply to the left, causing the door to slide shut.

I never got to eat the whole output of that nuclear reactor, but the part I tasted left me permanently transformed. I was and am now a better person than I had ever been. If only more people could taste what I tasted, the world would be a happier and better place.

When we got back to our former guest house, Jesus was waiting for us at the cantina. Based on the number of glasses lined up in front of him at the bar, He had been tossing back mescal with beer chasers for some time, but didn't seem any worse for the wear.

"You done us proud, kid. Nuclear power will be around for a long time thanks to you, and finally Monsanto GMO products are welcome all over the Third World. Yep, Armageddon is just around the corner. Want a drink?"

"I'd better not. I'm higher than a kite already."

"And you will be for some time. That stuff has a half-life of 25,000 years."

He was right. Ever since that day I have been feeling better than I can ever remember feeling before. Who needs Prozac when you have nuclear waste?

Veronica and I eventually returned to America, drawn by big money offered for my story. Turns out I didn't have to write it, there are people who will do that for you after just a Skype interview. Hallmark wanted to make a feel-good movie about it, featuring second tier actors who resembled movie stars, but without the distinct character of the more familiar prototypes. It would air many times on cable channels like Lifetime and Oxygen that appeal to middle aged women and offer stories of positive transformation.

Then came the interest in a real movie, an edgy affair directed by a German woman with an eating disorder who had made quite a name for herself in vampire erotica. She looked great from a distance, but up close she seemed an animated cadaver. Her husband, a little man who said nothing in the time I was with him, was scheduled to play me, except I heard there was also talk of offering it to Tommy Lee Jones, who had expressed interest. I was also informed that Kevin Spacey was considering the role of Dick Cheney, and Harry Dean Stanton wanted to flex his acting muscles with Nixon.

Even though nothing had really come to pass yet, I was now awash in money, and America seems a far more benign place when one need not worry about the cost of things. Suddenly, paying thirty dollars for lunch was normal. I spent more in tips than I had for food and services in Central America.

The old feelings of boredom returned, slowly at first, but then they accelerated. I was getting fat. I slept ten hours a day, and my biggest decision of each day merely involved which Netflix show to download. There was no reason to go anywhere, because all the shops were chain stores of some kind, and any personality they affected was contrived and artificial.

Most of the communications we received from Hollywood involved promotional tie-ins and merchandising. Would I be pleased to have an updated version of *Moon Rocks*, a fizzy fluorescently-colored candy that could be re-packaged as edible radioactive glass? All I need do is pose for the package portrait and the bucks would soon roll in. The part they were really excited about was the lack of necessary FDA approval, as the product had been approved years earlier after the Apollo missions.

Jesus sent word through his people that he would consider a feature role if one were written into the script of either movie. I instructed my people to tell his people we would try our best, but I knew that most of this was completely out of my hands. I wanted to ask him if he wanted to play a good guy or a bad guy, but feared maybe that would incur His wrath, and then I'd be in store for retribution mixed with mercy.

121

MEMO
Donald J. Trump

From: Henry Kissinger

To: Everyone on the List

It has come to my attention that a Reality TV star and somewhat shady real estate developer has political aspirations that may indeed work well with our ambitions.

His name is Donald Trump and he is, truth be told, not very bright. Nor is he virtuous, which may make him inclined to do our bidding when tempted by the standard lures that motivate most men.

If others in this group concur, I think we should go about contacting him using the standard inducements. Invite him to a banquet where other notables will make his acquaintance. Cigars, cognac, pretty women … the standard setting. Feel him out.

I think we may surprise ourselves with how easy this will turn out to be.

About the Scribe

Dan Coffey is a playwright, director and actor known for his work with Duck's Breath Mystery Theater and portraying memorable characters like Dr. Science. Dan lives in Chiang Mai, Thailand.